WALKING WITH WITCHES

LYNN HUGGINS-COOPER

Illustrated by Nigel J. Brewis

Tyne Bridge Publishing

Acknowledgements

Thanks to all those people who have been so generous with their time and knowledge, including staff at Newcastle Literary and Philosophical Society, and members of the Society of Antiquaries. Special thanks are due to Jo Bath and Barry Redfern, fellow Tyne Bridge authors, for letting me pick their brains. Thanks are also given to Bill Atkinson, caretaker at St Andrew's Church, Newgate Street, for his wonderful stories and atmospheric tour! Finally, thanks to Vanessa and Anna at Tyne Bridge for making the process fun, and to Nigel for his wonderful drawings. Finally, thanks to two groups of children: members of 'Educating at Home, Tyne and Wear' and the girls from 'Storm Writers' writing group. I would be lost without your comments.

Lynn Huggins-Cooper, 2008

www.walkingwithwitches.co.uk

The engraving on page 111 is from *England's Grievance Discovered in Relation to the Coal-Trade* by Ralph Gardner, 1655 (Newcastle Libraries collection). *Otherworld North East* by Tony Liddel is available from Tyne Bridge Publishing, PO Box 88, Newcastle upon Tyne NE99 1DX.

©Lynn Huggins-Cooper, 2008
Illustrations ©Nigel J. Brewis, 2008

ISBN: 978 185795 1288

City of Newcastle upon Tyne
Newcastle Libraries
Tyne Bridge Publishing
2008

www.tynebridgepublishing.co.uk

Printed by Athenaeum Press, Gateshead

For Kevin, Alex, Bethany
and Eleanor

'... mysterious and funny!'
(Rhanna, aged 12)

'I like the way there are funny
bits and really spooky bits.'
(Joe, aged 9)

'This book is really exciting ...
well scary!' *(Callum, aged 11)*

'I loved the scary bits best.'
(Beth aged 11)

The beginning – lights and shadows ...

Leaves skittered across the pavement, scratching along like brittle spiders. The wind toyed with them, lifting and whirling them into the air in spirals of orange and gold. Safe under the earth, something pulsed. Fingers of coloured light felt their way up towards the surface, stroking pebbles, buried coins and long-forgotten fragments of pottery. A curious mole was startled to feel his silky fur caressed by the warm beams of light. He shot above ground into air scented with wood smoke.

The coloured lights sparkled across discarded crisp packets and drinks cans as they blew across the building site. They paused over a coal black feather, illuminating it with green and gold. Overhead, a lonely crow cawed.

A dark shadow oozed towards the lights, attracted by their glitter. The darkness rolled across the ground like an oil slick, coating everything it touched with a greasy sheen. It slithered across the mole hill as the creature scrabbled backwards into the safety of its tunnel. The coloured lights froze, and then shot down a crack in the dry clay earth. Down through the layers that spoke of the history of the old town, through clay and stone, the light paused as it found the long dead bones of a small animal. It stroked the head, and then moved down the back to the place where a slinky tail had once twitched and swished. The bones shifted, subtly curling towards the light.

'Come, Skitterpaws... time for you to waken, my love. Danger draws near. We must search for the maiden who bears the blood of the sorceress. Only she can safeguard the Pendulum of Power – and only she can set us free.'

Chapter One

'Witches? What – you mean pointy hats, prone to cackling, close friends with toads?' Isabel laughed. 'I think you've got Halloween fever!' Eleanor pushed her friend. Cars rushed past, chased by trails of crisp packets and dry leaves. The old sandstone building loomed over them, casting the girls in deep shadow.

'No, stupid! Not Halloween witches with green skin and warty noses. Real witches. My dad showed me a clipping from the newspaper last night. They've dug up witches' bones in St Andrew's churchyard! Local witches – that's what we can do for our project!' Eleanor pulled a piece of paper from her pocket and pushed it into Isabel's hands.

'Ew! Sounds a bit gross... I'm not going ferreting about in any graveyards for mouldy old bones. Count me out!' She pulled a face at her friend. 'No way.'

'I'll change your mind...' Eleanor pulled a pencil out of her bag and waved it like a wand. 'I put a spell on you, and now you're mine...' she sang. Isabel flicked the pencil away and it flew into the air before landing in a huge stone plant pot like a tiny javelin. The girls collapsed into a fit of giggles.

'Right everyone! Quiet now... listen to me...' Mrs Price held up her hands and waited for the group to settle. 'Remember, the Literary and Philosophical Society building is a *library*. When we go inside, we must keep voices low and not disturb people working inside.'

A woman pushed open the heavy wooden doors of the library and stood behind Mrs Price on the steps. One by one, the teenagers were quiet, except for two girls who chattered on, oblivious to the silence around them.

'Erm… Izzy? Elle?' The girls turned to face Mrs Price, still shaking with laughter.

'Sorry Mum!' Isabel pulled a face and shifted from foot to foot.

'What I wanted to say, Izzy, is that the Lit and Phil are putting this session on especially for us. So we must be polite, and listen carefully…'

'And be *ambassadors for home educators everywhere* – we know!' Isabel and Eleanor chorused, putting their heads together, grinning and making angelic faces. Mrs Price turned to go into the library and bumped into the waiting librarian.

'It's lovely to meet you all!' the librarian smiled. 'My name is Caroline Grove, and I'll be showing you around this afternoon.'

'Oh! Sorry,' Mrs Price mumbled. 'I didn't realise you were going to meet us out here…'

'Come inside and I'll give you your tour – nothing too worthy I promise – and then you can explore on your own. Follow me.' Caroline turned and rushed off up the wide stone staircase. The entrance hall was lined with vast dark portraits. The librarian paused on the stairs.

'This is a portrait of Earl Grey, once Prime Minister – you can see him on the monument in the middle of Newcastle – and this is Robert Stephenson, who built the High Level Bridge. There is also a painting of Rev. William Turner, Founder and past Secretary of the Literary and Philosophical Society.'

'I thought she said it wasn't going to be boring!' Eleanor hissed. Isabel giggled and her mum poked her in the ribs, glaring. Caroline pushed open the heavy door at the top of the wrought iron staircase. 'Please – go on inside.' The group shuffled forwards into a large, high-ceilinged room crammed with books.

'Wow!' Eleanor breathed. 'It's like stepping back in time. Look at that balcony!' Above them, red ironwork jutted out into the room. The ceiling above was a confection of sugary white plaster topped with glass domes to let in light. 'It's beautiful!'

'We think so too.' Caroline nodded. 'I'll walk you round and show you the layout, and explain where you can find things. Then I'll give you your own map and you can wander round on your own and get a feel of the place. Now I'll show you the Sir James Knott room.' As they walked through the main room the smell of coffee wafted towards them.

'Mum'll be off for some of that in a minute, I bet you!' Isabel whispered. A group of elderly men sat in front of the tea hatch, chatting at a large library table topped with red leather.

'She'll have to fight her way past the granddad convention first!' Eleanor giggled. Caroline pointed at a series of tall book cases.

'This is the local history section, in the corner. There are many interesting old books here. I know your group is interested in carrying out some research for projects on local history, and this is a great place to start.'

'Think I'll stick to Google…' Isabel whispered. 'Hey – check out that spiral staircase. 'Bet you could have some fun sliding down that banister!'

'Right everyone! We'll pop downstairs so you can see the silent room and the lecture room. Then you're on your own, free to explore.' The librarian opened the heavy door.

'Hmm… I can barely wait.' Isabel pursed her lips. They followed Caroline down a stone staircase. 'More portraits, I see. Riveting.'

Caroline paused next to a tall pair of black doors. 'Usually, we would have to be silent in this room – hence the name! Today we have warned people that we are visiting.' She pushed open the doors. Cool air rushed over the group, and Mrs Price shivered. She raised her eyebrows and wiggled them at the girls. 'Spooky!' she mouthed.

'This is where people come to work quietly, when they need to concentrate. There are individual cubbies with desks, and we even have computer points for laptops now.' The room seemed dark and still. Pools of yellow light spilled onto the tables in the alcoves, making the main room seem gloomy.

'Not sure I'd like to work down here by myself,' Isabel stuffed her hands in her pockets. The group fell silent, and the only sound was the ticking of the huge wooden clock.

'Right everyone!' the librarian clapped her hands. Eleanor leaped in the air, her heart hammering in her chest. Mrs Price leaned close to Eleanor. 'Guess I wasn't the only one to find it spooky, eh?' she whispered.

'Sorry – I didn't mean to make you jump.' Caroline patted Eleanor's shoulder, and the girl's cheeks burned.

'Let's all go upstairs for a drink and a biscuit, and then I'll give you maps so you can explore for yourselves.'

'Where do you want to go?' Eleanor cocked her head on one side, unfolding the map. She traced the outlines of the rooms with her finger. 'Well, we haven't seen upstairs yet.' Isabel nodded, and pointed at the stairs. Grasping the map, the girls shot past the members only sign and up the winding staircase. The music room was full of scores, books and CDs. There were banks of honey coloured wooden catalogue drawers and a huge oval table with a red leather top.

'This is amazing! Some of these books are *really* old...' Isabel stroked a green leather spine embossed with gold leaf. Eleanor prowled round the room.

'Look! This white door is bolted and padlocked. Do you think it leads up to the attic?'

'So what if it does? It'll be dusty and boring.' Isabel shook her shoulders and flicked a piece of fluff off her jumper.

'Dusty? Hmm... I bet. An attic full of huge spiders, bloated with dust, and skeletons manacled to the walls, jaws clicking... moaning softly...'

'Ew! Shut up! It's probably just some old book store.' Isabel shuddered. Eleanor stared into the corner of the room, just over Isabel's shoulder. She turned her head as though she was tracking something moving slowly across the wall. 'Elle... stop it... I don't like it!' Eleanor's eyes flickered and she blinked hard.

'Just for a minute there, I thought I saw something...'

'I said *stop it*!' Isabel frowned. 'It's not funny!'

'I'm not trying to be funny. I saw... a shadow creeping across the wall behind you – and I couldn't work out where it was coming from, or what was making it move across the wall.' Isabel spun round to look at the wall, her eyes widening. Eleanor reached out slowly and ran her hand across the smooth plaster.

'It was weird… it kind of slid round the corner of the wall and slipped out onto the balcony. How…? Come on – let's go and have a look.' Isabel sighed, but followed her friend. 'It's probably just a trick of the light,' she muttered. Out on the balcony, Eleanor was staring down onto the ground floor of the library. She was rubbing her arms.

'Izzy, does it feel cold to you?'

'Well – yeah, but that's probably because we're out on the balcony in the open air.' Isabel pulled her jacket closed. 'It *is* getting colder… Elle…' she stopped speaking as her breath clouded white. 'What's happening? This isn't right. It's too warm inside for this…' Booming footsteps rang out on the stone staircase below them. 'Elle…' Isabel's eyes flooded with fear. Eleanor grabbed her arm.

'Come on! I don't even want to think about who *that* is coming up those stairs!' The girls shot along the balcony and clattered down the spiral metal staircase, round and round until their heads swam. The library was silent again.

'Who was it?' Isabel hissed. 'They should have appeared up on the balcony by now.' The girls craned their necks. At that moment, Caroline hurried down the staircase carrying a pile of books. Her heels clicked lightly on the stone staircase.

'Wasn't her then.' Eleanor whispered. 'Excuse me, did you see anyone up on the balcony?'

'Lost your friends? No, there's nobody up there I'm afraid. Perhaps they are in the silent room?' She wandered away pausing now and again to replace books as she walked.

'Explain *that*, then…' Eleanor frowned. The sound of heavy footfalls marched once more along the balcony above their heads. The girls peered up into the gloom. There was no one there.

Chapter Two

Late autumn sun poured in through the window, bathing the bedroom in pumpkin coloured light. Eleanor rolled over on the bed and rubbed her face with her hand. She reached out and stroked the sleeping cat who lay curled on the pillow. He stretched his paws and rubbed his head sleepily against her hand.

'Izzy... you know that weird stuff that happened last week, at the library... well, I know you think it was just because we were thinking about Halloween, but something strange happened that day. We were scared, and it wasn't just our imaginations working overtime.'

'What?' Isabel frowned into the mirror, where she was trying out purple lipstick. She pulled a face. 'Ugh – dead girl chic. Elle – you *really* have to think about a lighter palette.' Eleanor threw a scatter cushion at her friend. The cat jumped up and leaped from the bed.

'Maverick – don't be such a scaredy-cat!' She sighed as the cat stalked crossly from the room. 'Izzy, I'm trying to be serious! I'm talking about the stuff that happened at the Lit and Phil. The footsteps, the shadows – remember? I want to know what really happened.'

'Well, you know that I think we were maybe spooking ourselves because we wanted to be scared. On the way there we were talking about Halloween costumes and where we were going to go. Then Mum told us about local ghosts we could go as, like the Pink Lady of La Sagesse, remember? I think the stories all carried on filtering through and we were primed for being scared. We imagined it.' Isabel turned to her friend, scrubbing off the makeup with a tissue. Eleanor pursed her lips as she thought.

'Could be… but it seemed real at the time. You realise there's only one way to find out, don't you. We need to go back.'

'Go *back*?' Isabel grumbled. 'Apart from the spooky vibe, it's not exactly my idea of a fun day out…'

'We need to find more information on the witches for our project, too. We can look at the same time. And you have to admit it's exciting… a ghost hunt! We need to find out the truth.'

'We do? Can't we just agree it was a spooky experience and leave it there?'

'Not really.' Eleanor shook her head.

'I'm happy to forget about it. But you've got that look in your eyes again… I hate it when you get that look. It usually means I get dragged into something I'd rather just ignore and watch TV instead.' She sighed. 'Ok, I suppose I'll come. When though, Elle? We've got to plan our costumes. The Halloween Hootenanny is next week! We haven't got anything made yet – all we've got is our sketches. We need to get sewing! Luke's already got his Grim Reaper outfit, and Sarah's been making her wraith costume for weeks. She was showing me – there are loads of layers of net and she's hand painted it with greys and greens – it looks amazing. Lily and Hermione are going as demons, and have been sewing glittery scales on their costumes for ages. India and Tabitha showed me the zombie masks they're making – complete with a glass eye that hangs out on the cheek! We're going to end up looking really lame at this rate.'

'Well, we can get on with that later. Since there's no time to lose, we'd better go this afternoon!' She jumped off the bed and started pushing her friend towards the door.

As the bus pulled into Central Station, Eleanor leapt up, pulling Isabel out of her chair and straight into an elderly man waiting to get off. She sprawled across a double seat as she tried to avoid him.

'Elle! Oh – sorry… I didn't mean to bump you. My friend… '

'No problem! It's not often lovely young women fall at my feet.' The man beamed. He put out his hand and helped Isabel up. 'There you go, my dear!' He tapped the brim of his hat and gestured to the door. 'After you, ladies!'

'Thanks… sorry!' Isabel muttered, and rushed to the front of the bus.

Eleanor giggled. 'I'm sorry too.' She shot after her friend. 'Think you scored a hit there, mind – that's your date for the Hootenanny sorted!' Isabel punched her arm.

'Steady on!' Eleanor rubbed her arm. 'I said I was sorry! Anyway – there it is. Let's go inside and see what we can find out!'

'If we *must*…' The girls pushed through the double doors and went up the staircase. The library was busy. A large table was surrounded with older men reading papers and gossiping.

'I see the granddad posse are still here. Do you think they went home after we saw them last week?' Isabel snickered.

'No… I reckon they flock into the basement and hang there like bats until the librarians come into work on a morning and disturb them!' A tall thin man stood and put his hat on, flapping his dark coat out behind him. 'See! Told you!' Eleanor giggled. 'Anyway, let's ask the librarian if she's got any books about the history of the library.'

'Elle – look. *This book might help*. It's called *Otherworld North East*. I bet it's got some ghost stories in it that'll help us sort out our costumes too!' Isabel was waving the book at Eleanor. 'I'll have a look while you ask.'

'Great idea, Izzy! Hey look… ' she pointed at a poster. 'It says it's only £10 for junior members. You fancy joining? It might help us with our project.'

'Oh… Elle… does that mean we'll be coming here a lot?'

'Well… it's a lovely library anyway and you know our mums will give us the money – education and all that!'

'Oh… OK… ' Isabel rummaged in her backpack. 'Lead me to it.' she pulled out her purse. The librarian at the desk was Caroline, who had shown them around on their trip.

'Hello girls! Lovely to see you back again. You must have enjoyed your tour! And wanting to join – fabulous.' She gave them a sheaf of forms to fill in. 'If you put your names and addresses here, I'll sort out your tickets.' She pulled out a file and minutes later handed the girls their library cards and receipts. 'Here's a map of the library – but of course you know your way round already! Is there anything else I can help you with?'

'Actually, there is. Do you have a history of the library, by any chance?' Eleanor asked. Caroline bustled out from behind the desk and picked up a book from the table by the entrance.

'Here – this should tell you what you need to know. If there's anything else, just ask.'

The girls thanked the librarian and found a table to read at. Eleanor leafed through the history book and Isabel flipped through *Otherworld North East*.

'No way. Absolutely *no way*!' she breathed. 'Elle – you're not going to believe this – this place is supposed to be haunted. There's even a ghost upstairs in the music room… ' her eyes widened. 'It's a witch finder! They had a vigil here and he *made himself known.*'

'Like – by rushing around upstairs frightening girls?' Eleanor asked, her eyes bright. 'Do you think he knew what we'd chosen to do for our project? Perhaps it was a warning… ' Eleanor clawed her fingers and wiggled them at Isabel.

'Give over! My money's still on shadows and our overactive imaginations.' Isabel looked over her shoulder and shivered.

'You have to admit it's one hell of a creepy coincidence though. Anyway, let's get these books out so we can look at them at home. I want to have another look round now.'

The girls wandered round the library. Isabel stuck her woolly hat on the marble bust of Robert Stephenson. 'Suits you, sir!' Eleanor smirked, and looked at the display case in front of the statue.

'Hey – look, Izzy. This old book is supposed to have belonged to one of our witches!' the display case held a book bound with embossed leather, with delicate pages covered in elegant copperplate writing in coloured inks. Small pen and ink sketches illustrated the pages.

'Look at that crow – it's great! Corvus,' Eleanor read, peering at the faint inks. 'Do you think that was his name?'

'I guess so. Lovely book, isn't it? Bet your mum would love it!'

'Oh yes – we'll have to bring her in and show her. Hey – listen to this:

Element of Air, I call you here. Blow the winds of change and cleanse this space of the growing darkness.'

A cool breeze ruffled Eleanor's fringe.

'Element of Fire, I call you here. Burn through the darkness and light the way.

Element of Water, I call you here. Cleanse this space and make it safe.

Element of Earth, I call you here. Shelter and hide your children from the evil that stalks us. Blessed be!'

Eleanor looked up. 'Heavy stuff, eh?'

'Elle... those pages are flickering... how is wind getting in there?' Izzy peered through the glass.

'Um... ' Eleanor felt round the edges of the case. 'There are no gaps... '

'So how is it moving? Elle?' Isabel stepped back. Eleanor touched the cold glass and bent forwards. She frowned, and then sniffed deeply.

'Izzy? Can you smell something spicy? It smells a bit like… Christmas! You know, that mince pie and Christmas cake smell – cinnamon and apples. Weird.' Eleanor rubbed her forehead.

'Elle – those pages are turning by themselves, look!' The girls stared as the delicate pages fluttered quickly past, like the wings of a moth hovering near a flame. They slowed, and the book fell open at a page with a sketch of a tabby cat and an inquisitive crow, its head cocked on one side. Eleanor read aloud.

Beltane 1649. I have sent my beloved Skitterpaws and Corvus hence until this coming darkness passes. They will be safe on my brother's estate, though dear Alexander himself is absent on account of this wretched war. Darling Charlotte, my niece, will love Skitterpaws as her own and it pleases me to think a kind hand will stroke and feed her. And Charlotte was ever amused by the antics of Corvus as he begs cleverly for food. I shall miss them so, but like my treasures, my darlings will be safer hidden.

She turned to Isabel, her eyes sparkling. 'I think it's a message, maybe from one of our own witches! Look at the label!' A carefully typed card lay next to the book, which read 'Ellenor Henderson, executed on the Town Moor Newcastle upon Tyne in 1650.'

'What message though? It's a bit late to ask us to feed her cat…' Isabel joked shakily.

'I know this is freaky, but think about it carefully for a minute.

Why did this happen to us? Is this witch trying to ask for help? She mentions her hidden treasures. What if she wants us to find them again?'

'Surely, if she hid it, she didn't want it to be found.' Isabel frowned. 'Hey – you've got me as daft as you! I'm talking about this as if it was real!'

'But Izzy, you saw the pages move. Do you have any other explanation for that?' Isabel's eyes slid away from her friend's piercing gaze. 'Perhaps she hid it from *someone in particular*. She was frightened of something – or someone. Look – she talked about 'coming darkness' and sent her pets away because she thought they were in danger. Izzy, I think she wants us to go treasure hunting!' Eleanor grabbed her friend's arm.

'I hate to put a dampener on this Elle, but even if you are right – we don't know where to look.'

'Well – not yet, but I bet we can work it out. Imagine – it could be a hoard of coins and jewels!'

'Or a bag of dried frogs, a broken wand and some mouldy herbs... ' Isabel sighed.

'Oh, OK... well, let's start by looking online and see what we can find out about our witch. We have a name – with the powers of the Internet at our fingertips we won't need magic! It can't be that hard.' The girls huddled over the computer. A frustrating hour later they were still there. Isabel kicked back in her chair. 'I thought it was easy to find things out on the computer. Usually all I do is type my subject into Google and the information pings out at me. We're getting nowhere.'

Eleanor pursed her lips. 'I think we might have to do this the hard way.' She pushed her fringe out of her eyes.

'You mean hitting the books, right?' Isabel raised her eyebrows.

'That's right. Let's start with the local history section. It's in that room over there – the Sir James Knott room, I think Caroline called it.' She pushed imaginary glasses up her nose as she mimicked the librarian. '*It's a wonderful collection.* Well, if that's the case, it should have what we need.' Isabel's shoulders slumped. 'Come on then – we'd better get started.'

The books held some amazing stories.

'Look at this one.' Eleanor turned the book to look at the spine. '*The Borderer's Table Book Volumes 1-2*, no less.' She leafed through the pages of the book, and started to read. '*1650, 21st August. Thes partes her under named, wer executed in the town mor for wiches* – it includes a list of the witches' names, and there's an Isabell Bown – an Isabell, Izzy! And there's the Ellenor who wrote the journal.' She ran her finger under the list of names. Somehow, I'm beginning to think that's not a coincidence. They share our names – or we share theirs. It's a link, you know?'

'Bit of a vague one.' Isabel frowned. 'Anyway, I don't know about you, but I'm ready to leave all this for a while, and get some lunch. If we go up to the Arts Centre cafe on Westgate Road I can call into the shop. I need some charcoals for a new project.'

'Yeah – that's great.' Eleanor pushed the books back into place on the high shelves. 'What's your new project?'

'Well, it's funny but I've been fancying a large scale sketch of a crow – not just because we saw one in Ellenor's journal, either, before you jump to conclusions! I've been thinking about it all week. There have been loads hanging round the stables near us lately – huge things. Really funny to watch too. They bounce around like black feathery balls yelling and croaking at each other.

Take that look off your face – I know what you're going to say before you say it. *Perhaps it's an omen of things to come…* ' she swept her jacket round her shoulders and drew herself up to her full height. '*Beware old ladies bearing shiny red apples, my dear!*' she cackled. Eleanor smiled, but as she walked into the shadow of the balcony on her way to the door, she felt as though iced water was trickling down her back.

Chapter Three

The rain beat down on the roof of Haymarket bus station, playing a rhythm with watery fingertips. Eleanor stared through the glass at the street beyond. Since last week's visit to the Lit and Phil, she had been unable to sleep. Rumbling buses pulled in to the bus stands leaving plumes of exhaust hanging in the air. People jostled for space, creating a warm soupy smell of damp wool and wet skin. Eleanor slumped back in her seat, watching single raindrops as they joined forces and ran together in channels down the windows. The lights in the bus station shone on the wet glass, breaking the drops into tiny rainbows.

As Eleanor stared, the water formed a pattern. Her nose wrinkled as the smell of sun-warmed apples surrounded her. She watched spellbound as water swirled to make the shape of a face, framed by heavy locks of hair. It looked back at her from the glass, with eyes that brimmed with tears. A mouth grimaced in pain, and began to move as it spoke. *'Help us... help us... help us...'*

'Did you want this bus, love?' Eleanor jerked forwards and banged her head on the glass. 'I think you were dropping off there! Too many late nights, eh?' Eleanor gazed at the young woman who had spoken, bewildered. The strange vision faded. She shook herself, smiling shakily and waving her fingers at the toddler staring up at her from a grubby buggy. Stepping on to the warm bus, she settled and pulled out her mobile phone. She tapped in a familiar number, and as the call connected she let out a breath she hadn't realised she was holding.

'Izzy – something really odd just happened!' she leaned her head against the cool window.

'Elle? Is that you? What's wrong?'

'I... saw a face at the bus station.'

'Well, that's not a newsflash. They do tend to be busy places, you know! Was the face cute, by any chance? You do sound a bit breathless!'

'No – I'm not kidding, Izzy. This is going to sound mad, but... the face... it was made of water! It was a woman. She looked really scared, or in pain. She kept saying "help us," and tears were streaming down her face.' There was a pause at the other end of the line.

'Elle... no-one is listening to you, are they?' Eleanor jerked the phone away from her face, looking at it as though it had bitten her.

'You don't believe me, do you? There's nothing wrong with me. I saw her. She was real! And something else – I could smell apples again, you know – just like at the Lit and Phil!'

'Ok, calm down. It's not that I don't believe you or anything. I believe you saw her – I'm just not sure if I believe she was actually *there*. Sorry, Elle. Are you sure it's not just you thinking too much about our project? Listen, I know you were going to stop off on the way over to buy the beads for our costumes, but why don't you just come straight here? We can talk about it and see if there isn't an explanation for these things.' A smile entered her voice. 'I have chocolate... come on, you know you want to... ' Eleanor slumped in the chair.

'OK, Izzy. But it happened. The woman was real. I think it's all linked with our witches, you know? She was trying so hard to talk to me… and she was begging for help.'

In Isabel's kitchen, over a cup of hot chocolate heaped with squirty cream and marshmallows, Eleanor tried to explain the events at the bus station.

'I was watching the rain on the window and her face just kind of morphed out of the drops. I could smell apples again, as though it was the middle of summer… and the scent reminded me of last week when the book flipped pages in the Lit and Phil, you know?' She peered into her cup and picked out a sticky pink marshmallow. 'She looked in such pain. It really freaked me out.'

'I'm not surprised! Now, don't get mad with me, but… I'm worried about you. I've seen all the stuff you've been collecting – the books from the library; print-offs from the Internet. It's all over your bedroom. You're getting a bit obsessed, Elle… ' she touched her friend's arm. Eleanor looked up, and Isabel jumped as she saw the bleak look in her eyes.

'She's real, Izzy. You've got to believe me.' She gripped her friend's hand. 'I can't get over the feeling that if we don't help her, something terrible will happen.'

'Have you talked to your mum about this, Elle?' Isabel frowned.

'Hardly! You can just imagine – she'd think I was loopy and would never let me out of the house again! No, this is something we need to do ourselves – I can feel it. I think we need to put some real effort into finding that treasure mentioned in the witch's journal. I can't stop thinking about it, and every time I think about it, I feel kind of … itchy, inside.'

Isabel pulled a face.

'I just don't think this weird feeling – and the strange things that are happening – will stop until we find the treasure.'

'Well, it all sounds a bit like something from one of those silly graphic novels you like reading. But if it means this much to you, I'll help. I don't like it, and I'm not saying I believe that there is anything *remotely* magical going on here – but I'll help because you need me to.'

'Thanks Iz – just knowing I can share this with you helps.'

'Well, we can think about it and see what ideas we come up with.' Isabel squeezed Eleanor's hand. 'In the meantime, let's keep you busy with something else. We can have a go at sorting out these costumes, for a start – it's only a week until Halloween!'

The week passed slowly. Every night, Eleanor woke from nightmares that drifted around at the edges of her mind. She felt drained, waking each morning to feel as though she had spent the night running, searching for something that stayed out of reach. By Halloween, she felt as though she was wading through a swamp. Her legs felt heavy, and it was an effort to stay awake.

Dusk fell on Halloween, covering the town like a grey cobweb. Eleanor was so tired that she could barely be bothered to put on her costume. She sat on the bed, watching listlessly as Isabel painted sparkling green make up around her eyes.

'Are you OK, Elle? Sorry to sound like my mum, but I hope you're not coming down with something. You've been so quiet all week.'

'I'm really tired, that's all. I keep having nightmares and waking up scared. It's awful. Then during the day, I feel really jumpy – you know, like something bad's after me. It's the dreams leaving me feeling... *off*... ' Eleanor sighed.

'Poor you!' Isabel frowned. 'Hmm... I know what will cheer you up! Come here and I'll do your make up. It'll be time to go soon.' Eleanor rolled her eyes, but sat down in the chair ready for her friend to paint stars, moons and glitter on her face. When the make up was finished, Eleanor stared at herself in the mirror. She looked pale and tired, but somehow older.

'Every inch the powerful Sorceress!' Isabel flourished the brush she held in her hand. 'Time to go – Dad's hovering. He wants to watch the footie in the pub, so he needs to dump us before kick off!'

As Eleanor stood, she felt the tiredness seep out of her. Walking down the stairs, she shook her hair and her head cleared. When she stepped outside into the pale moonlight, she felt as though energy and light were filling her, pouring down from the sky.

'Hey – you look better already!' Isabel smiled. 'I told you – make up always makes you feel better!'

The journey to the party took them through streets filled with small goblins and witches clutching their mothers' hands. Gangs of sheet-covered ghosts and masked zombies roamed from door to door, filling bags with sweet treats. Soon, the car pulled in to the kerb by the university. The Hootenanny was being organised by students, and a headless spectre waited by a door festooned with orange and black crepe streamers.

'Enter... if you dare!' the ghost boomed. Then he spoiled the effect by asking for their tickets.

'Hmm… very spooky – *not*!' Isabel frowned.

'Be nice, Izzy!' her dad laughed. 'Have fun, girls – I'll be here to collect you at 10.30. Once you're inside, stay inside, remember?' Isabel nodded and waved.

'Bye dad! Yes – that means go!' she giggled.

Inside, the room was decorated with black silken webs, and torn netting covered the doorways. Jack o' lanterns clustered on tables and window sills, filling the gloom with their eerie orange glow. A tall vampire was handing out punch.

'*I vant to suck your blood…* '

'Hmm… in your dreams, Count Dorkula!' Isabel snorted. The girls took a glass of juice each and wandered round the room.

'Hey – look! Here's India and Tabitha – *gross*!' Eleanor flicked a dangling glass eye on India's mask. 'That is truly foul – I love it!' she giggled. She jumped as a glittering purple demon poked her with a pitchfork.

'Nice costumes, girls.' Lily and Hermione twirled to show the full effect of their costumes, from horns to long, slippery tails.

'Oh – wow – these must have taken you weeks! All these lovely sequins and beads… ' Isabel stroked the scaly costumes.

'Greetings, mortals.' A beautiful wraith fluttered past, waving fingers that ended in glittering grey nails.

'Sarah – that's stunning. I love it!' Isabel sighed. 'See – I told you everyone would show us up if we didn't get moving… ' she hissed into Eleanor's ear. 'Bet you're glad you listened now! And there's Patrick… and Catherine… and Nell… *great ghoul costumes, guys!*' Isabel waved.

'Where's Luke though? He said he'd meet us here.' Eleanor frowned. A white hand curled over her shoulder. Bony fingers grasped her neck and she shrieked, whirling round and pushing the creature away from her. It tumbled to the ground and lay there groaning. Eleanor leapt backwards, her eyes wide.

'Izzy… it's… it's… '

'Luke. It's *Luke*, Eleanor. For goodness sake – *get a grip!*' Isabel rushed across to pull the figure to its feet. Eleanor looked at the long black robe, and saw familiar grey trainers sticking out of the bottom.

'Oh, Luke – sorry – you made me jump! I didn't mean… ' Eleanor flushed red.

'Well, it's OK. I probably asked for it anyway!' Luke brushed shining Halloween confetti off his robes, and a hail of purple bats twirled to the floor. 'What do you think?' He wafted his frayed costume backwards and forwards. 'Grim enough?'

'Totally!' Eleanor poked his arm. 'You certainly spooked me!'

The group of friends wandered around the room, stopping now and again for snacks. The ghouls raced up and down, leaping in front of people and dancing weird dances. The demons bobbed for apples with the wraith. Isabel sighed.

'This is getting a bit lame. I thought it was going to be really great, being at the university and all that… but it's the same old people doing the same old stuff. I wish we could go somewhere less *predictable*. Somewhere truly spooky, instead of a room full of people we know doing what they always do.'

'Oh – it's OK, Iz. I mean – it's not like there are any alternatives, are there?' Eleanor bit into a biscuit in the shape of a severed finger. Jam dripped onto her chin, like blood.

'Well, I was thinking... ' Luke pushed back his hood and scrubbed his fingers through his spiky hair.

'Steady on, Luke! Did it hurt, you – thinking?' Eleanor giggled. Luke stuck out his tongue. 'Why don't we go for a walk round the town and scare a few people?'

'Well, because we promised my dad we'd stay here for one thing; for another, that sounds *totally* lame!' Isabel frowned. 'And the weather doesn't look so good. I don't want to ruin my dress...'

'I know somewhere we can go to scare people as they go past – where they are building the new library. Loads of students go past there on their way back to halls. Come on – it'll be great!'

'Well, it's not that late, Izzy. It might be fun... I mean – the streets are still full of people because it's late night shopping. It's not like we are creeping around in the dead of night or anything. We can be back here before your dad comes to pick us up. Come on – let's have a bit of fun.' Isabel chewed her lip. 'OK.' She sighed. 'But I get the feeling I'm going to regret this... ' *At least it's getting your mind off the witches*, she thought to herself. *And that's got to be worth getting a bit damp...*

The three friends slipped out of the venue. They ran down the street, shrieking and laughing. An old lady frowned at them as they shot past her. 'Silly kids! You could've had me over!' she called after them. Luke ran ahead, calling out apologies. Eleanor spotted an alley and pointed to it silently. The girls shot down the narrow lane.

'At this rate, we'll beat him there! I'll teach him to try and scare me – you'll see!' Eleanor panted. 'There it is!' In front of them was a huge space filled with piles of stone, wood and pipes. Machinery stood idle in the darkness of a locked compound, like dinosaurs frozen in time.

'But why are we here? This is just a building site.' Isabel grumbled.

'You were the one who said the Hootenanny was lame. You wanted to go somewhere, and I quote *truly spooky*. Well, this fits the bill, doesn't it? Dark, abandoned, dangerous... what's the problem?'

'It was lame. Bobbing for apples – in this make up? I don't think so! Well, I'll grant you it's dark out here, and it's abandoned because the workmen have gone home – but it looks muddy and sticky rather than spooky. Trust Luke to race off somewhere stupid like this.' Isabel wrinkled her nose. 'I can't see the point in trailing about here.' A rustling sound came from a pile of stones. 'And if there are rats, I'll never speak to you again, Eleanor... '

A dark figure loomed out of the darkness. Isabel grabbed Eleanor's arm. 'What's that?'

'It's probably just Luke trying to put the frighteners on us. *Luke! We can see you! Come here!*' The figure hesitated, and then drifted towards the girls. A pale hand beckoned to them. 'Luke – cut it out. You're not going to scare us again, you know.' Eleanor ducked under the metal barrier. It rocked, and clanged a metallic warning.

'Elle... I'm not sure we should be here. I don't want to drag this sorceress costume through the mud – it'll be ruined.' She stroked the purple velvet gown.

'Oh – come on, Izzy! If we don't go through Luke will think he scared us – and he'll never stop going on about it. *Luke – we're coming*. Where's he gone?'

Isabel sighed and slipped under the barrier. 'Ok… don't know why this place is supposed to be so interesting though – it just looks like a pile of rubble and mud to me,' she grumbled. Eleanor stood in the middle of the site, turning her head.

'*Luke! This is getting stupid…* ah! There he is!' Eleanor broke into a run, chasing the dark robed figure. As she got closer, she saw that the robes were forest green, studded with beads and silver painted symbols. She stumbled and fell, grazing her hand on a chunk of concrete. She sucked air in sharply through her teeth as beads of blood began to well out of the wound. Isabel caught up and bobbed down next to Eleanor.

'Ooh – that looks sore! Are you OK?' She pulled a hankie out of her pocket and patted Eleanor's cut gently. 'Where's Luke gone?'

'Izzy, I don't think it was Luke. He was wearing black, right?'

'Regulation Reaper-wear, yes.' She darted glances round the dark site. 'Elle, if this is a wind up and Luke jumps out I swear I'll… '

'No, no it's not. When I got closer, 'Luke' was wearing a green robe covered with beads and stars… and then I fell. When I looked up again, he was gone – whoever *he* was.'

'Right, that's it. We're getting out of here.' Isabel tugged at Eleanor's uninjured hand. Eleanor pulled back as she tried to get up. She slipped and her hand slapped the ground. Her fingers dug deeply into the softened earth of a molehill. She pulled her hand out of the soil and saw a metallic glimmer.

'Izzy – I think I've found something.' She scraped at the soil and found the hard corner of a small wooden box. 'Help me – it could be something important!'

'If you think I'm scratching about in the dirt after it took me half an hour to paint the patterns on my nails, you're sadly mistaken. I want to go, Elle.' She looked over her shoulder into the darkness. Eleanor looked up at her friend. 'It could be treasure, remember! Jewels and gold... and if you help, the box will come out of the ground quicker – and we can go – promise!'

Isabel sighed theatrically and knelt down next to Eleanor. She lifted small stones out of the way between her finger and thumb. Eleanor scrabbled at the dirt, faster and faster. Strips of rotten cloth fell away from the sides of the box. 'It must be really old... look, the lid has carvings on it.' Eleanor ran her finger gently across the exposed lid. Starlight gathered overhead, cascading down onto the box, and surrounding the girls in a silver glow. The light slid around them like cloaks, electrifying their hair. Eleanor tugged, and the lid of the box flew off with a pop. The scent of apples filled the air.

'Oh, wow... look at this stuff!' Eleanor had levered the box out of the mud. She tipped the contents into her hand. Pewter coloured coins, strange round bells and a necklace, blackened with age sat in her palm.

'There's something else in there, Elle – look!' Isabel pointed at a lumpy package, wrapped in brown paper. Eleanor picked it out, and some of the paper flaked into the box. Isabel picked up a fragment. 'Look, it has drawings and some sort of writing on it.' She held the paper out to Eleanor. Spidery script, strange symbols and stars covered the paper. Eleanor carefully peeled the paper open. Inside, there was a chain that ended with a stone that still glittered, despite its muddy coating. Eleanor pulled her heavy velvet skirt aside and rubbed the crystal on her jeans.

'Jeans?' Isabel asked. 'Since when did a Sorceress wear jeans under her robes?'

'Since now. I hate wearing skirts, and this felt a bit more comfortable. Look, Iz! It's some sort of gem stone. Strange though; it's on a single chain, so it can't be a necklace, unless it's broken.'

'Ha! That'll teach Luke to abandon us – we found something amazing!' Isabel looked behind her. 'I still keep expecting him to leap out on us though.' She stood up, stretching her legs. 'Come on Elle – let's go. I can't see Luke any more, and this place is starting to creep me out. We can have a proper look at the treasure at home.'

'*Treasure…* that's what it is! Ellenor's treasure!'

'*Eleanor's?* Erm – I think we both found it!' Isabel said sharply. Eleanor looked confused. 'Ah, no – I wasn't saying *Eleanor's* treasure – *Ellenor*. The witch. *Our witch*. Hey! Maybe that's who the figure in green was – the witch from the book, remember?'

Izzy stared at Eleanor. 'Did you bang your head when you fell?' she sighed heavily. 'Come on. It's cold and damp, and I want to be back before dad comes. Luke's probably there already, laughing at us.' She pulled Eleanor to her feet and started to hurry towards the barrier, looking behind her every few moments. Carrying the box and its contents against her chest, Eleanor followed her friend, scrambling across the building site. Back on the brightly lit main street, late night shoppers bustled past them with heads bowed against the drizzle that had started to fall.

Chapter Four

Back at Isabel's house, Eleanor sat down on the guest bed and rummaged in her bag. She pulled out the box, and gently unwrapped the stone.

'Hang on – my leg's buzzing!' Isabel patted her pocket. She pulled out her phone and frowned. 'It's a text from Luke. He says he's sorry, but he twisted his ankle on the way to the building site and had to ring his mum to pick him up. So… if Luke had gone home… '

'Who was that we were following? Weird… ' Eleanor frowned and shrugged. 'Oh well. Let's give this a wash and have a good look.' She went into the bathroom and ran warm water into the sink. She squirted soap into the water and gently swished the muddy gemstone through the bubbles. As she wafted the chain backwards and forwards, small plumes of muddy soil peeled away from the surface. She stroked her finger across the gleaming stone.

'It feels warm!' she muttered.

'Well – duh! It is in hot water… ' Isabel wrinkled her nose. Eleanor pulled the stone from the water and carefully patted it dry.

'Well – it doesn't look broken.' Isabel murmured. 'Look – it's got a ring on the end. Do you think it's supposed to hang from something?'

'Maybe. It reminds me of something. It's a bit like those hanging crystals for the window – the ones that make rainbows?'

'There are some lovely crystals in the window of that shop in

Eldon Square. That one with the dragon models and crystal balls, you know? We could go and have a look tomorrow when we go into town and see if there are any there like this one.'

'Sounds like a plan!' Eleanor held the chain and the gemstone dangled, turning in slow circles. Her smile slipped as the stone spun faster, pulling against her. She wrapped it quickly and pushed it back into the box.

'Shall we make some hot chocolate?' Isabel stretched and yawned. 'We've got fudge flavour… or dark mint, and we've got some chocolate fingers to help it go down!'

'It all sounds good to me. I feel a bit cold, actually.' Eleanor rubbed her arms.

'It must be all that ferreting about in the mud.' Isabel sniffed.

'Yeah – but it was worth it – look what we found!' Eleanor clapped her hands.

'True… but I'm still glad to be home now, safe and warm. Come on – chocolate's calling!'

Down in the kitchen, Isabel flicked the switch on the kettle and grabbed mugs from the rack. Eleanor stared out of the window as the kettle heated. A breeze blew in through the window vent bringing the scent of the fallen apples on the lawn. She breathed deeply, enjoying the sharp fragrance.

'Hey, dreamer – spoon some chocolate into the mugs while I put these biscuits on a plate, will you?' Isabel held out the tub of chocolate powder. Eleanor took it and put heaped spoonfuls in each mug.

'I'm just getting some marshmallows for the hot chocolate – stick the water in the mugs, will you?' Isabel was rummaging in the cupboard.

Eleanor added the water and stirred the drinks, watching columns of steam rise into the air. Deep in thought, she continued to stir long after the chocolate powder dispersed. She stared into the mug, watching the liquid whirl in a circle. It seemed to Eleanor that she was staring down a dark tunnel which filled her vision. A strange pulling sensation forced her to watch as shapes formed in the liquid. Her eyes widened as fingers groped out of the dark tunnel, and a hand reached towards her like a pale starfish.

Isabel touched her shoulder and she leapt in the air.

'Hey – I was going to say that there's a spooky old film about to start on the telly, but you seem jumpy already! It won't be too scary though, and it will make a perfect end to Halloween – it's got vampires *and* werewolves! We can watch it in my room. I've put the snacks on the tray there. There are even some cute little chocolate pumpkins. Bring them up, will you?'

'Sorry, Izzy. I was miles away there! Tray... yep – got it. Lead on!' The girls clattered up the stairs, and Isabel switched on the television on the stand above the bed. Settling down in piles of pillows and blankets, the girls were soon lost in a world of misty moors and lonely old castle ruins.

The next morning, the girls packed the box they had found carefully in a rucksack and got the bus to town. 'That's the place!' Isabel pointed. 'The Dancing Goddess.' The shop window was full of crystals. Faeries sat on chunks of pink rose quartz; jewellery was draped across spiky pieces of glittering purple amethyst. A huge crystal ball sat on a star covered stand in the centre of the display. Sparkling beads hung from a gothic black tree across the corner of the window, throwing shards of rainbow across velvet

cloaks and lace gloves. Brightly coloured tarot cards lay spread on silk cloths, and embroidered Goddess dolls lounged on chunks of driftwood.

'I can see plenty of crystals, but nothing like ours.' Eleanor patted the bag. 'Come on, let's have a look inside.' Perfumed oils and incense filled the air inside the shop with spicy smells.

'Wow! Look at these skirts. My mum would love them… ' Eleanor stroked the velvet folds. Tiny bells jingled as the fabric moved. Isabel picked up a chunk of dark green rock.

'Malachite, so the label says. Very pretty – but expensive!' she put the stone back on the shelf. She wiggled her eyebrows at Eleanor. 'Oh look – there's a book about crystals. That might tell us something about our find.' Isabel pulled the heavy book down from the shelf and started to flip the pages. 'Hmm… lots of lovely crystals, but nothing like ours.'

'Can I help you, girls?' A smiling woman with long brown hair stood behind them. 'I'm Kelli. Merry meet and welcome to The Dancing Goddess. Are you looking for a particular type of crystal?'

'Oh! Thanks! We actually have a crystal, and we are trying to find out what it is, exactly. Do you think you could help us?'

'Of course!' the woman nodded. 'Rhanna! Can you come and help?' A pretty, smiling girl pushed a curtain aside and stepped into the shop.

'What is it, Mum?'

'These young ladies have a crystal they need to identify.' She turned to the girls. 'My daughter is very good with crystals. She can identify just about anything, and knows exactly which crystal you need for a purpose!'

'I've washed it, but it's still a bit mucky.' Eleanor rummaged in her bag and pulled out a stained wad of tissue. 'Here... ' She unwrapped the crystal and dropped it into Rhanna's hand. The chain slithered across her fingers, leaving behind a trail of loose soil.

'Oh wow! Mum – look at this! It's wonderful.' She held the crystal out to her mother. The woman took the chain between her thumb and forefinger. The crystal dangled, spinning slowly in a circle. Her face shone.

'Girls – this is a very special crystal indeed. I feel honoured to see it. Where did you get it?'

'We... erm... found it. Dug it up, really.' Eleanor mumbled. Kelli smoothed the chain with her fingers, her nail polish sparkling green in the light of a nearby lamp. Isabel touched the crystal gently with the tip of her finger.

'We thought it might be a necklace, but broken, you know? Then we thought it might be one of those crystals you hang in the window to catch the light.'

The woman's head snapped up. 'Oh – it's much more than that! What you have here is a pendulum, my dear. A very, very old pendulum, if I'm not mistaken.'

'A pendulum? What's that?' Eleanor asked.

'A witch's tool of divination!' Kelli beamed. Isabel and Eleanor looked each other, and back to the crystal.

'What Mum's trying to say is that a pendulum like this would have been used by a witch to answer questions, or to find things – even to see the future. People still use them today. We have some in the window over there.' The girls walked over and saw a collection of gems on chains. Some were plain quartz points; others were ornately decorated with pearls and tiny jewels.

'They're beautiful… ' Eleanor whispered.

'Here – take a leaflet. It helps to explain what the pendulum is used for.' Kelli caught hold of Eleanor's fingers. 'You know – I'm not sure a magickal tool this powerful could be found by just anyone.' She narrowed her eyes and peered into Eleanor's face. 'I think, my dear, that maybe it found you.'

'Sorry?'

'Well, I'm sensing that this pendulum belonged to a very powerful and wise woman. A witch like that would have set wards and protective bindings upon her tools if she hid them. They would be too powerful to be allowed to fall into the wrong hands. I think they called to you, and that's why you found them.' She rubbed her hands together. 'Doesn't the very thought of it make your hands tingle? Can't you feel the power, the warmth of the pendulum flooding into you?'

Eleanor darted a look at Isabel. 'Warmth!' she mouthed.

'Oh, this is so exciting! We must look into this further. Oh, I'm so glad you came to me girls! It's such an honour to be involved. Come along – let's sit and have a drink and a chat. Some herbal tea? Cordial?'

'Erm… no thanks – we're not thirsty right now, thanks. We have to get going… sorry. We have to be somewhere. Thanks for your help.' Isabel grabbed Eleanor's arm and steered her out of the shop. Eleanor stammered a goodbye over her shoulder. Isabel continued to push Eleanor as she walked quickly down the busy street.

'What a freak!' she laughed. 'I couldn't stay there for another minute without laughing in her face – and I didn't want to hurt her feelings, even if she was weird. Come on – we'll get a frappucino. My treat!' Isabel hurried Eleanor down the steps into the cafe.

'She wasn't that bad!' Eleanor laughed.

'Hey – let's sit there, in the corner. Check out the Hellfire!' Isabel grinned. Eleanor looked round the cafe. Glittering red flames licked up the wall and a witches' besom hung over an archway. The smell of coffee and caramel syrup swirled around them as they sat down in leather armchairs.

'Wow! She was totally *beyond* bats in the belfry! Can you believe that? Her poor daughter… I thought my mum was embarrassing!' Isabel slurped her drink.

'I thought she was really nice.' Eleanor frowned. 'And I think there might be something in what she said, you know?' Isabel leaned forward in her seat. 'Elle – some daft *New Age* hippy woman is the last thing you need right now. You're already too tied up in this witches project. You don't need anyone encouraging you.'

The door swung open and Rhanna rushed in to the cafe. She scanned the room and waved as she spotted the two girls.

'I thought I saw you come in here! I thought you said you weren't thirsty? Mum can come on a bit strong sometimes… sorry about that. But she really can help you. She can seem a bit batty, but she really knows what she's talking about!'

Isabel stared down at her shoes. Eleanor tried to hide her smile. 'Here – come and sit with us. You want a drink? Izzy's paying.' Isabel slid off towards the counter to order. 'I thought your mum was great. It's just… a lot of weird, scary things have been happening lately. It's a lot to take in. Sorry if we seemed a bit rude, rushing off like that. I hope your mum wasn't upset.'

'Not at all! She's back there pulling cartons of books out of the cupboard to find some information for you. Once she gets her teeth into something, she just doesn't let go. She thinks this pendulum could be a very important find, and wants to help you. She kept saying that you would need spells of protection to keep the pendulum – and yourself – safe.'

Isabel came back to the table with a raspberry smoothie and put it on the table in front of Rhanna. 'Look… I'm sorry we rushed off like that… I was a bit… '

'No worries. My mum can get a bit intense, but she's not as strange as she sounds at first meeting!' Rhanna sighed. Isabel flushed pink. 'Your friend here has been telling me that some scary stuff has been happening, and my mum knew somehow, and wants to help. I know it sounds weird, but she's really good at what she does. Please let her help you.'

'That would be great, Rhanna.' Eleanor nodded. 'There's a lot going on here and some of it is hard to understand. We need all the help we can get! When we've had these drinks, we're going to go back to the library and see if we can find out any more about our witches.

'We are?' Isabel moaned. Eleanor frowned. 'OK – we are.' Isabel sighed. 'I'd better have a bit of that chocolate brownie then – I need the energy!' She rushed over to the counter to order. Eleanor stared into the distance.

'It's OK, Eleanor. I know it all seems a bit scary at the moment, but my mum will be able to help you, I promise. Try not to worry.'

Rhanna smiled. Eleanor looked bleakly into the other girl's eyes.

'Oh Rhanna – I hope so. I really hope so. At the moment I just don't know what to believe. All I know for sure is that I'm scared of what's going on. I feel as though I'm going nuts at times.' She scrubbed her hand in her hair and leaned on the table. 'Izzy's trying to help, but I know that at times she thinks I've lost it. The thing is, I'm not sure that I haven't either... ' She sat up straight. 'But the best way to deal with something is to find out more about it – so back to the library!'

Isabel dumped a pile of cake bars and sweets on the table. 'There – confectionery goodness – just the thing for a long afternoon hitting the books. I got a brownie for you too Rhanna. Hey – you'll never guess what – they had a tray of *spell bags* on the counter! With all these witches coming out of the woodwork it looks like The Dancing Goddess might have some competition!'

'No, it doesn't work like that. Think about it – doesn't that give you proof that magick is everywhere, even where you don't expect to find it? My Mum always says 'The Lady works in mysterious ways' and I think this would be an example. You need the protection magick can offer, and suddenly you find yourself surrounded by spell weavers. What could be better than that?' She sat back in her chair and folded her arms.

'An afternoon shopping in Fenwicks?' Isabel put her head on one side. 'A day at the dentists having fillings?'

'Izzy!' Eleanor smirked. Rhanna cackled, and then batted Isabel's knee.

'Well, I'd better get back to the shop. Mum has a past lives class this afternoon, and she wants me to watch the shop for her. Good luck with the books!' She swiped a brownie from the table and ripped the wrapper with her teeth. 'Thanks, Izzy. See you later!'

Eleanor stood as Isabel pushed the cakes and sweets into her bag.

'You ready, Iz?'

'Ready as I'll ever be. Come on, the sooner we get going, the sooner we can go home and watch the telly.'

As the door swung shut behind the girls, the woman behind the counter pulled out the large silver pentacle she wore round her neck and kissed it.

'Goddess, protect her. There's a dark shadow attached to that girl, and I fear for her.' She patted the spell bags on the counter. 'And I fear she'll need something a bit more powerful than *you* to help her!'

Chapter Five

The Lit and Phil was quiet, apart from the rustling of pages and the hum of rain on the glass-domed roof. Isabel's eyes wandered round the room as she sipped a glass of juice. She ran her finger round the rim.

'Elle, I still don't think it's too late to change our project, you know? We could do it about the slave trade – you remember that exhibition we went to last year?' Isabel leaned across the library table and patted her friend's arm. Eleanor's head shot up.

'Sorry? Hey, Iz – this bit is really interesting... but kind of sad. Did you know that at the time when our witches were executed, you could be suspected of witchcraft for all sorts of stupid reasons? This book says that a witch was identified because she wore a red waistcoat and a green petticoat!'

'Hmm... if clothes make you a witch, there's no hope for Rhanna's mum and her mates then!' Isabel laughed. Eleanor pushed her friend and made a face.

'I'm serious. Can you imagine living in a time when women – and even some men – were called witches because of what they wore, or the cures they helped people with? There weren't doctors for poor people, so wise women would help with herbal remedies – and if they annoyed someone, or somebody didn't get well, they could be accused of witchcraft! In those days it wasn't name calling – it ended in torture and death.' Eleanor's eyes glittered suddenly with tears. Isabel frowned.

'This is exactly why we need to change our project. You are getting in way too deep, Elle. You keep getting upset. I really think we should stop.'

'Stop? We can't *stop*. Ellenor needs our help. I had a weird dream last night – no, Izzy – listen to me. I was in her garden. I was wearing a long green dress made from soft wool, and I was carrying a basket. I was pinching dead heads off flowers and clearing away broken twigs. A tabby cat was circling my feet, rubbing her warm head against my ankles. I knew I was collecting herbs to make a … *tincture*… for Widow Marlowe. She had something I called *the ague*.' Eleanor rubbed her forehead. 'But then something happened to scare me and I can't remember what!'

'Elle – it was just a dream, you know? This is exactly what I'm talking about. You are getting so obsessed that you're even making up dreams about witches! We need to forget about it.'

'But Izzy, I had to look up *tincture* and *ague* in the dictionary this morning – I didn't have a clue what they were! I didn't make this up. It was as though somehow in the dream I actually *became* Ellenor.'

'Oh, Elle – this is beyond being obsessed. Do you know how mad this sounds? Even weirder than Rhanna's mum the other day!' she crossed her arms and sat back in the chair.

'Izzy – of course! We can go back and see Rhanna's mum again! She'll help me to understand what's going on.' She jumped up, scattering books and papers. 'Help me put these away, will you?'

Isabel stood still. She stared at her friends, her arms crossed. 'Elle – I really don't think we should do this. I think you need to forget about the witches – even if they were witches – and especially Ellenor. I am not going to help you get into this any deeper. I won't go to see some mad old hippy who will convince you you're seeing the *Lady of Avalon*, or whatever!'

'Well stay here by yourself then, because that's where I'm going right now. Where people listen to me, and don't treat me as though I was mad. Thanks for the lack of support, Isabel.' She grabbed her bag and ran down the stairs into the street.

In the library, a dark oily shadow coiled down from the balcony, and swirled around Isabel's shoulders. She pulled her collar tighter round her neck, and the shadow moved on. It slithered down the staircase and billowed into the street in a cloud of dirty grey smoke.

Eleanor rushed up the road and pushed open the door of The Dancing Goddess. A group of women were clustered round the jewellery display, admiring gemstone necklaces and pendants.

'Eleanor! Lovely to see you again so soon.' Kelli emerged from the group and swept towards her. She hugged Eleanor, who found herself enveloped in a cloud of patchouli. 'Rhanna told me she had seen you in the coffee shop. But you look worried. Come – let's have a cup of cardamom tea to clear our minds and we can wrestle with your problem!'

Eleanor followed in Kelli's wake, and found herself in a cosy kitchen. A huge black cat sat on the table, lolling on a pile of papers.

'Down, *Mr Loki!*' Kelli pushed the cat onto the floor. 'Sorry, Eleanor... still, what would tea be without a few cat hairs!' she giggled as Rhanna came into the room.

'She is joking, honestly! I'm guessing the library wasn't as helpful as you hoped, huh?'

Kelli took a large copper kettle off the hob and poured water into a black tea pot painted with stars and moons. She added a packet from the shelf, and as she stirred the pot the air was filled with a warm spicy scent. She poured out a cup of tea and put it in front of Eleanor.

'Now, have a seat and tell me all about it. You have been having dreams, yes?'

'Yes... how did you know? I keep having weird dreams, where I see places I know I have been, they are so familiar – but I don't recognise them. That sounds mad.' She rested her head wearily on her hands.

Kelli patted her shoulder. 'I'll tell you what – can you tell me a little about what you have seen? I could make some notes, and we could see if they give us any clues.'

Eleanor sighed, and sipped her tea. 'OK... anything that will help. This is starting to take over my life! I can't think of anything else.'

'I'll fetch a notebook. When you've finished your tea, we'll go through into the garden room and you can relax and get comfortable. Then you can tell me what you remember and I'll get it down on paper. Don't worry, my love. We'll get to the bottom of this!'

The garden room was light and airy, and the door opened onto a courtyard filled with pots of billowing lavender and spiky rosemary. Loki slithered past Eleanor, stroking his tail against her leg. He settled himself on a clump of thyme and promptly fell asleep.

'Sit here – it's the most comfortable chair.' Kelli held out her hand towards a wicker seat piled high with cushions. Eleanor sank into the chair. 'Breathe deeply and enjoy the scent of the herbs. I get them all from a lovely place at Ebchester called The Herb Patch. Have you been there? It is wonderful – such a place of power! The Romans sensed it and built a fort there. I swear the power from the soil is taken in by the herbs as they grow. Rhanna and I must take you there some time! Anyway, rest yourself, and try to clear your mind. It will help you to relax.' Eleanor sat back and closed her eyes, breathing deeply. The sound of a blackbird singing swirled around her, washing the tension from her body. She breathed the warm scent of the herbs and allowed herself to relax. A cat rubbed around her ankles. *Mr Loki is trying to help*, she thought, smiling to herself. Dappled sunlight flickered across her face, making patterns of orange on her eyelids.

'You are happy and safe, Eleanor. You are completely relaxed.' Kelli lit a stick of incense and the pungent smoke coiled into the air. She rang a small bell, and the clear sound seemed to swell and bounce off the walls in an echo. 'I call upon Green Tara, fierce and loving Goddess to protect you and centre you as you search for answers. Green Tara, bring Eleanor swift wisdom and a quick mind, and make her fearless.'

Suddenly, Eleanor found herself in a garden. A tabby cat rubbed round her legs and then ran in circles like a furry dervish. It chased petals blowing down from a rose bush like confetti, batting them with velvet paws. A glossy crow cackled down at her from the branches of a gnarled old apple tree, and the leaves rustled soft applause.

'Skitterpaws! Settle down!' Ellenor called. The cat stared at her balefully, circled twice, and flopped down in a clump of meadowsweet. A cloud of perfume rose from the bruised leaves.

'That is better!' She stroked the cat and bent down next to the hedge to clip herbs into her basket. Footsteps came down the dusty lane past the garden and chattering voices floated across the hedge.

'Careful! Don't pick those berries – them'll be poisoned! That's Mistress Henderson's cottage. You know her's a witch!'

'Hush yourself, Jennet! You should be ashamed of that sort of tattle! You know that kindness is the only thing Mistress Henderson has ever shown you and yours! Remember when your Peter had a face like a pudden because of a gumboil? Who lanced the nasty thing and made poultices to soothe and heal the ache?'

'But Bella! Everyone knows her uses charms and spells. When Polly's baby was born blue and cold, Mistress Henderson were helping at the birthing. Polly's mother said she grabbed the still baby and put her mouth over his and sucked the evil spirit right out of him! He choked a breath and pinked right up. Tell me that sort of power is not witchcraft!'

'You really are a ninny! Mistress Henderson is a healer. She is too good a soul to have any truck with the dark arts. She is a goodwife, pure and simple. Stop this tattle – you never know when evil ears are listening.'

The footsteps started again, rushing off down the lane. As the voices faded into the distance, still arguing, Ellenor bit her lip and reached over and stroked the cat's silky head. 'Ah, Skitterpaws… the stories are growing, fuelled by fools and encouraged by the wicked. They'll have me turning into a cat and dancing with Old Nick himself next!' She laughed, but the sound was brittle and ended in a sob. She hid her face in the cat's warm fur. 'We live in dark times, my love, and we must be cautious.'

Chapter Six

'Eleanor? Breathe deeply and try slowly to pull yourself back to this time, and this place. Use my voice as a beacon... follow my voice... and here you are! How are you feeling, my dear?'

Eleanor sat up and rubbed her eyes. 'I... I... ' she croaked.

'Here, have a sip of elderflower cordial. That always perks me up. Rhanna made it herself. It's very good. And take one of these lavender shortbreads. I find a little nibble always grounds me when I have been travelling.'

Eleanor nibbled absently on a biscuit. Her mouth was filled with the sweet taste of sugared lavender flowers.

'Travelling? What do you mean? I had the dream again... I must have dropped off.' She rubbed her face.

'Eleanor, I made notes of what you were saying. We've been in here for about an hour. Rhanna's been watching the shop for me, along with Emma who comes in the afternoons so I can get on with my sewing and crafting for the shop. Would you like to tell me what you remember from the dream so we can see if our stories are the same?'

'An hour? Surely not – I just came and sat down a few moments ago.'

'Don't worry about that. How about you run me through the dream again, while it's still fresh in your mind?'

'Well, I was... she was... ' Eleanor frowned. 'I don't know – it was like the woman was me but not me if that makes sense? It was like it was me, looking out through her eyes. Wow – that sounds stupid!'

'Not at all. It's much more common than you'd think. Now – go on with the dream.'

'I was in my garden – well not my garden ... the woman's garden, and I was picking herbs, and watching the cat... and the crow... ' Her head shot up and she stared at Kelli, wide eyed. 'Skitterpaws – I called the cat Skitterpaws. That was Ellenor's cat. I was... I was... the witch. The witch I have been studying. We saw the name in the book in the library. Ellenor's book. There were people talking by the hedge and they couldn't see me, and I knew I was in danger... or soon would be.' Her eyes brimmed with tears, and she scrubbed at them with the back of her hand. 'I'm babbling. You must think I'm very strange – sorry, I'm usually quite sensible.' She tried to smile, but her lip wobbled. Kelli came and bobbed next to her chair, patting her hand.

'Don't worry, Eleanor. All this can seem strange, and scary, but you are not alone. Rhanna and I will help you.' She squeezed Eleanor's hand. 'What I think is happening is that you are somehow... channelling this wise woman, Ellenor. Her memories are somehow being passed through you. This is going to sound very odd, but I read my tarot cards after you were here last time. I think you are tuning in to the memories of the wise woman who owned the pendulum. There must be some sort of connection between the two of you... I don't know what... but I think the pendulum is acting as a type of *psychic TV aerial*, if you like. It is allowing you to see through her eyes. I think she may be trying to tell you something.'

The curtain separating the shop and the flat shifted and tiny bells jingled. 'Mum?' Rhanna called from the kitchen.

'We're in here! Come through.'

Rhanna came into the garden room, followed closely by Isabel.

'Look who's here!'

'I came to find you... I knew you would be here, and I was worried. Not because you were here, I mean!' Isabel wrinkled her nose and grimaced. 'Sorry – let me start again! Elle – I just wanted to find you and check you were OK.'

'I'm fine. And I'm sorry I snapped at you earlier. I'm fine... Kelli has been trying to help me sort out my thoughts.'

Kelli stood up. 'We'll come back to my notes next time, Eleanor. I think you need a rest now. Isabel – will you join us for a drink?'

'I'm OK thanks – we have to go home now because my mum will be expecting us for dinner. She gets a bit freaky when we're late!'

'We mothers just want our daughters to be safe – it's a common sort of *freakiness*, isn't it Rhanna?' Kelli patted her daughter's head.

'Tell me about it!' The girl nudged her mum.

Kelli rummaged in her desk drawer. 'Here, Eleanor. Take this postcard. It shows Green Tara. Pop her on the wall by your bed, and focus on her as you fall asleep. Ask her to protect you as you dream, and she will come to your aid. And there's something in the shop I want you to have. Come through with me girls.'

Kelli swept through the curtain into the shop and lifted what looked like a green and black web down from a hook on the ceiling. Iridescent black feathers, glittering beads and tiny shells dangled from the bottom of the web.

'It's a dream catcher, Eleanor. Hang this over your bed and it will help to sift out the scarier parts of your dreams. The beads are labradorite. This crystal helps to reactivate ancient memories… especially those that are relevant to our own spiritual growth. And this green crystal point is aventurine. It is an excellent protection stone, and blocks negative energies that would try to tap in to your soul. These are crow feathers, which echo the crow that called to you in your dream. The crow is a powerful, magical bird which has powers to protect and banish evil. The feathers will sweep away anything dark or negative that draws near to you.'

'Mum! *Please*. I think Eleanor has had enough for one afternoon!' Rhanna frowned at her mother.

'Sorry, sorry… getting carried away again! Here, let me wrap it in tissue for you.' Kelli pulled a sheet of silver tissue from the counter and quickly wrapped the dream catcher, securing the package with a length of black ribbon. 'I shall keep you in my thoughts, Eleanor. Do come again soon!' she handed the package to Eleanor.

'I… I will. Thanks, Kelli.'

'Um… Rhanna, Elle and I are getting tickets to see *NightStalker* at the Sage. We were wondering if you'd like to come too?'

'Hey – that would be great! They're one of my favourite bands! Is that OK mum?' Rhanna asked.

'It would be fine.'

'OK – I'll get the tickets tomorrow. See you later!' Isabel

pushed open the shop door.

'Take care, girls. We'll see you again very soon. Don't forget to hang up the dream catcher… '

The bell above the door jangled as the girls went out into the street. Kelli rubbed her arms.

'Mum? You OK?' Rhanna put her arm round her mum's shoulders.

'I'm fine… just concerned. There's a dark cloud following that girl, and I can't make out what it is. I hope she hangs that dream catcher above her bed.'

'I'm sure she will – it's great. Really pretty, and probably one of your best ever.'

'When I was making it, you know, I wove in powerful spells of protection because I knew they'd be needed. I picked the beads specially, and as I tied on the feathers I knew I was using them to act as a conduit – a pathway. The crow's feathers do fight negativity, but they have another function. The crow carries messages from the dead. At that time, I didn't know why I was using them. Now, I think I do. Rhanna, when your friend was having her vision – it wasn't a dream, it was a powerful vision – I was watching her. Her features… *shifted*. I saw another woman shimmering beneath the surface. I believe it was the spirit of the witch, Ellenor Henderson.'

Chapter Seven

On the evening of the *NightStalker* concert, Rhanna was waiting in the lobby when Isabel and Eleanor arrived.

'Hi there! Sarah rang my mobile before – she's going to be a bit late. She'll meet us inside, she said.' The girls made their way into the hall, music blaring from the stack of amps by the stage. Moments later, they saw Sarah weaving through the crowd as the lights dimmed. The crowd roared as the lead singer took the stage, and the guitars built into a wall of sound. He flicked his blond hair behind his shoulders, and tipped his head back and stared at the roof, waiting to sing.

'Oh wow!' Isabel shouted over the noise. 'Listen to that guitar!'

'Sorry – I'd been stuck in traffic so long, I had to go to the loo before I came in. Those toilets are miles away!' Sarah grumbled. 'And the queue is ridiculous. There's some opera on in the big hall, so there were swarms of grannies with too much *bling* fighting for mirror space!' The singer grabbed the mike and the girls were soon part of the crowd surging backwards and forwards across the dance floor.

'This is our last song. You've been a great audience, Newcastle!' He wiped his face with a cloth and threw it into the crowd. Isabel shot forwards and grabbed it, stuffing it in her pocket. She grabbed Sarah's hand and started pulling her backwards into the crowd.

'Did you see that? Did you see? I caught it!' Her face shone.

Sarah stuck out her tongue. 'Blah! A sweaty hankie… *great*. I wish I had one too… ' Isabel pushed her friend and made a face. The crowd moved slowly towards the exits.

Eleanor waved at the *ladies* sign. 'I must use the loo before we go. Tell mum I'm just coming or she'll think I've been abducted or something. I know – you can tell her about your sweaty hankie – I'm sure she'll be impressed!'

Eleanor made her way through the crowd, and pushed open the heavy doors. The toilets were empty and silent. She hurried in and out of a cubicle. Somewhere nearby, a door slammed and she jumped. She quickly pressed the taps and the water gushed over her hands. She rubbed them over her sweaty face and scowled at herself in the mirror, shaking her head. 'What is wrong with me…?' she muttered. 'It's just quiet because everyone's going home… ' She glanced at the room around her in the mirror. The black walls seemed to suck in light, and her own pale face shone back at her from the darkness. She grabbed a paper towel and blotted her face quickly, closing her eyes. The air changed suddenly, pressing against her face like a balloon. Her eyes flashed open wide. Looking back at her from the mirror was her own face, overlaid with another. Dark blue eyes mixed with green; shining red hair mixed with blonde. Eleanor reached out to touch the mirror, and the other hand reached back at her. Instead of cold glass, she found herself touching warm flesh. Strong fingers closed around hers.

'Please… help me. My need is great, or I would not ask. There is great danger, and darkness follows you closely. It watches you as a hawk watches a wren… '

The face in the mirror shifted. Dark tendrils began to coil at the edge of Eleanor's vision. The face in the mirror closed its eyes and gritted its teeth.

'I shall not allow it! By the Lady, begone!'

The image in the mirror raised her hands and spread her fingers. Silver light shimmered and crackled around her, and the darkness faded like smoke, drifting away into nothing.

'He is close. I feel the chill of his presence drawing near. I shall protect you, but you must be wary. He would have the pendulum and seeks to take it from your care. Guard it well or all is lost... '

Eleanor struggled to speak. Her mouth felt gummed shut.

'I know I ask much of you... you are so young, but I would not ask unless I knew you were the one chosen as Guardian. In my time, that duty fell to me and shaped my life – and my death. I do not seek to alarm you, but you need to understand the grave, dangerous task that lies before you. When darkness overwhelmed me, I had already hidden the pendulum. I rose before the sun and hid my box of treasures in my herb garden. I guarded it with wards and sigils, and the day they came to take me, they could not find it. The witch finder – or he who took the form of the witch finder – tortured me but I would not reveal its whereabouts. More than my simple life was at stake. It remained hidden down the centuries and the shape-shifter followed it, searching endlessly down the years. Down the ages, this demon has drawn on magickal power sources like the pendulum to free himself to walk the earth once more, and destroy all that is good. He draws close. The wards I set upon the pendulum sensed the threat and triggered a call to you – the Guardian. You must not allow him to have it or all that is good and true shall be lost... '

The image flickered like a bad TV transmission.

'*I shall come to you again, when I can… beware… watch for the dark shape-shifter… he means you harm.*'

The image faded and died.

'Wait!' Eleanor shouted and lurched forwards, her head bouncing off the glass as she hit the mirror hard. Isabel stuck her head round the door.

'It's OK – we're still waiting, Elle – we didn't want to face your mum without you! Hey! Are you OK?'

'I… er… bumped my head.' Eleanor stared into the mirror.

'I saw! You look a bit spaced, Elle. It's quite an egg you've got there. No wonder you look weird. Let's get you back to your mum.'

'Izzy… I saw something… someone.' She scrubbed at her eyes.

'Hey – you don't have a concussion, do you? If you do, your mum'll never let you out again. And if you're not allowed out… I won't be! Our mums have some kind of pact, I think.' She shook her head. 'Turn to the light a minute, Elle – let me look at your eyes. I did first aid, remember.' Eleanor shrugged off her friend's arm.

'Will you listen to me for a minute! This is really important! There was a woman… in the mirror. And the pendulum feels warm.' She reached into the neck of her T shirt and pulled the pendulum into the light. It was glowing.

Chapter Eight

The girls looked at each other, their eyes wide. Isabel reached out her hand and touched the pendulum with her finger.

'It feels really hot! Way hotter than your skin could've made it, even in the heat of the crowd in the hall. That is so weird... '

Eleanor tucked the pendulum back inside her T shirt.

'I know. Listen, don't tell the others about it just yet, will you? I want to think about this for a bit without having to explain it to anyone.'

'Are you sure about that? Don't you think we ought to tell your mum?'

'At the moment, that's the last person I want to talk to about it. She'd get all freaked out, and might even stop me from going to The Dancing Goddess. I need to be able to talk to Rhanna's mum about this and can't see my mum being keen. You know she'd want to explain everything rationally – a bit like you!' she nudged her friend.

'I'd still like to do that – it's just that I'm starting to think it can't be explained that easily.' She sighed. 'OK – but if it gets too scary, we have to tell someone. But I can't see that a few more days can make a difference.'

Outside, Eleanor's mum was waiting in the car park. The beams that lit up the Baltic art gallery glinted on the river, sending shoals of golden lights swimming across the water. Rhanna and

Sarah were already in the back of the car.

'Good concert, girls?'

'Great thanks!' Isabel beamed. 'And I caught the singer's hankie!'

'Hankie? Did he drop it?'

'He threw it into the crowd. I shall keep it forever!' she mock swooned into the back seat of the car.

'How about you, Elle? Did you have a good time? You're a bit quiet.'

'Great thanks mum. I'm just tired. It was really hot in there.'

'OK. Right – we'd better get *mum's taxi service* on the road! Rhanna, I'll drop you first since you're in the town, then Sarah. Izzy, you're sleeping over with us, so we can go straight home after dropping Sarah, and I can watch *Gardener's World* – I taped it earlier so I wouldn't miss it.'

The girls chattered on the way home, but Eleanor leaned her head against the cool glass window and stared into the darkness. Pinpricks of light twinkled in the valley as they drove up the hill towards home.

'Hey, sleepyhead! You're not being very sociable. It's a good job Izzy's not shy with me. You've hardly said two words since you got in the car!' They pulled up on the gravel outside the house.

'Sorry. I was just thinking. Come on Iz – I'll make some hot chocolate and we can take it upstairs. You want some, mum?'

'No thanks – I'll just settle myself here and watch my programme. There are blankets and pillows on your dresser. Sleep well!' She turned to the television and the girls heard Monty Don talking about the importance of *a good thick mulch* as they walked into the kitchen.

'Riveting stuff for oldies, obviously!' Eleanor whispered. Isabel giggled. Grabbing a pack of biscuits and two mugs of chocolate, the girls went upstairs.

'Are you really OK Elle?'Isabel asked as she fussed with blankets and pillows.

'Yeah… I'll be fine. I just need to get things straight in my own head.' The girls climbed into their beds.

'I see you hung the dream catcher on the wall. It's really pretty. So how do we know if it's working? Do you wake up in the morning and find it full of old bits of frayed bat wing and the odd dry spider leg, sieved out of your nightmares?'

'Nothing quite so exciting. I just hope it keeps the bad dreams away. I truly am tired, and could do with a good night's sleep. I keep waking through the night with my heart pounding.' Eleanor rubbed her eyes.

'Well, I'm in here tonight – and I'm sure I can keep the bad dreams away. I'm really quite fierce, you know!' Isabel bared her teeth.

'Well, you scare me!' Eleanor snuggled into the blankets. 'Night, Iz.'

'Night Elle. Sweet dreams.'

As she slept that night, Eleanor found herself in the garden again. It was dark, and pearly light drifted down through the trees, washing her face with silver. Her hands were digging in dark soil, which trickled through her fingers like brown sugar. A tabby cat mewed anxiously.

'Fear not, Skitterpaws. I shall bury the casket deeply. It can stay here until the danger has passed.' She stopped to stroke the tabby's soft ears.

'Mrrew?' The cat pawed at her skirts.

'Yes, beloved. It shall pass. And you will not be away for long. We shall leave this night. I must know you and Corvus are in safety, then I can concentrate on the task to come.'

A lonely crow cawed overhead, circling in the darkness and throwing a shadow across the moon. Ellenor patted down the soil and strewed leaves across the newly dug patch.

'That will help.' She placed a smooth pebble etched with a mark scratched on the surface on the mound of earth. 'A sigil of protection to mask this resting place. And now we must journey to my brother's house. Come, Skitterpaws. Corvus will follow.' She looked up at the sky and frowned. 'There's a halo round the moon tonight – so a storm is brewing.' She closed her eyes and sighed. 'Goddess, I beseech you – guard us and keep us safe from the storm.' She picked up her tools and, with the cat following, she went into the house and put on her heaviest cloak.

Under her duvet, Eleanor rolled over and moaned. A dark shadow flitted past the bedroom window, and Isabel stirred and frowned. The wind buffeted against the side of the house, moaning as it poked its fingers under roofing tiles and tried to prise them off.

On a dark hillside, Ellenor pushed on through the night. The rain beat down to soak her woollen cloak which slapped muddily round her ankles. She carried a large closed basket with a howling cat inside. Above her head, a crow could be seen with each flash of lightning. In the distance, the dark shapes of the approaching village were outlined against the sky. Her heart was as heavy as her sodden feet as she trudged on through the gloom.

'We draw near, my loves. A safe haven beckons you. Take heart!' she called.

Back in the stuffy bedroom, beads of sweat stuck Eleanor's hair to her face, but she pulled the covers tightly around her neck as though she was frozen. A shadow slipped into the room through a crack by the window, crept across the floor and across the wall. It coiled around the dream catcher and started as it touched a crystal. It trembled, then slid down onto the bed. It travelled towards Eleanor's head and hovered above her face. She murmured in her sleep, and curled her lips as though a terrible taste had crept into her mouth. She spluttered, and then gagged as the shadow coiled slowly around her neck. Out in the garden, a vixen shrieked and Eleanor sat up suddenly, staring at the window.

'Shape-shifter, begone! You have no hold over me!' she shouted. She raised her arms above her head and opened her palms, then clapped her hands. Isabel shot out of bed.

'Whassit? Elle? You OK?'

Eleanor stared blankly out of the window.

'He was here... ' she closed her eyes and slumped down onto the bed. Isabel tucked the duvet around her friend's shoulders and patted her arm.

'It's OK Elle, it was just a bad dream.' She switched on the reading light. 'I'll leave that on, just in case you wake up again.' She shivered, and her eyes searched the dark corners of the room.

She shook herself and reached across to flick the dream catcher. 'Fat lot of use you are!' she muttered. She turned to walk back to her bed, and out of the corner of her eye she saw a shadow cross the window. She decided not to look outside.

Chapter Nine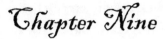

The next morning, Eleanor felt drained. She could barely drag herself out of bed.

'Morning, Iz,' she mumbled.

'Wow! You look shattered. I guess the nightmare took its toll, eh?'

'Nightmare? Did you have a nightmare? It didn't wake me… '

'Me? Well – I'm surprised I didn't have one after your performance! You were moaning and groaning, and you shot up in bed and shouted that there was a *shape-shifter*, whatever that was – and it didn't sound good. Can't you remember anything?'

Eleanor pushed a hand through her hair. 'I can't. Isn't that strange?'

'So the dream catcher doesn't work then!' Isabel nodded her head towards the web. 'Hey – what's that?' she reached up and poked the threads. A piece of dull metal hit the dressing table with a *thunk*. Isabel picked it up and turned it over in her hand.

'I don't remember this being there before.' She frowned. She offered it to Eleanor.

'It looks like part of a signet ring – my dad has one a bit like this. I think this is really old. I wonder what these marks mean?'

The broken ring had an image scratched into the face.

'It looks like crossed keys… or maybe swords.' Eleanor rotated the ring in her hand. She dropped it suddenly and put her hand to her mouth.

'Ow! It cut me!' As she peered at her hand, a bead of blood bloomed from a tiny cut on her palm. 'It didn't look sharp!'

'You'd better wash that and put some cream on it. An old thing like that could be swarming with germs!' Isabel frowned. As Eleanor went to the bathroom, Isabel picked up the ring with a hankie and pushed it into a drawer. She shivered, and rubbed her arms. When Eleanor returned, she was staring out of the window.

'Hey Elle – I never thought I'd say this, but I think we should go and ask Rhanna's mum about the ring. There's something weird going on here and I think she's the only one who won't think we're nuts if we ask. We'd better take the ring.' She tugged the drawer open and pointed at the hankie. 'It's there.'

Eleanor pulled on her jeans and a black *NightStalker* T shirt. 'Why is it in… ? Well, grab it then. I can smell fried breakfast going on downstairs – so let's go down and see what there is. Then we can go into town. Thanks, Iz.'

'Thanks for what?'

'For getting involved in this with me.'

'Like I have a choice!' Isabel tugged on her jeans and vest.

'Elle – you get the ring, will you?' she flushed red. 'I'd rather not touch it.' Eleanor grabbed the hankie and stuffed it into her bag. She slung it over her shoulder.

Downstairs, plates of eggs, tomatoes, beans and toast waited for them. The girls wolfed them down and jumped up together, pulling on their trainers.

'That was great, thanks!' Isabel burped. 'Oops! Pardon me!'

'Yep – nice one, Mum! We're off to the library to do some more research on our project, and we're going to call for Rhanna first, OK?'

'That's wonderful dear. It's really great to see how keen you both are. I can't wait to see the finished project! I'm going to get some work done while you're gone – I have an article about *green nappies* to write and the deadline's this week.'

'*Green nappies*? Ew – gross!' Eleanor held her nose theatrically.

'You know fine well that I mean *eco-friendly* nappies, you beast!' She flicked Eleanor with the damp tea towel she was holding. 'Go on – get away with you and stop tormenting your poor mother! See you at lunch time.'

The girls ran and caught the big orange bus for town just as it started to pull away from their stop. As it pulled into the bus station, they stood up. Eleanor fiddled with the pendulum absent-mindedly.

'You know, when I woke up this morning, the pendulum had left a mark on my skin. It was as though it had got really hot in the night. Not just warm from my skin, but actually *hot*, you know?'

Isabel pursed her lips. 'Well, I don't know what's going on. I don't even pretend to understand, but we'll get to the bottom of this. And even if I think Kelli is a bit crazy, I'm beginning to think she knows what she's talking about. And the stuff that's going on is so bizarre… well, it's going to take *weird* to fight *weird*, if you know what I mean!'

The Dancing Goddess was full of people. Kelli saw them across the crowd.

'Girls! Hi! I'll be with you in a moment. Our 'make your own runes' course is just about to begin, and I'm settling the students with Emma.' She circled her hands at the group of women who surrounded her. 'Go through – Rhanna's at the table in the kitchen, writing in her journal.'

In the kitchen, lentil soup simmered on the stove. Rhanna was stirring the pot as they pushed through the curtain from the shop.

'Hi there! I was just talking about you. Great concert last night – I really enjoyed it. That lead singer… ' she sighed happily. 'How are things? You look a bit tired, Elle. Did you stay up talking all night?'

'Actually, she had terrible nightmares. But she kept me awake most of the night!' Isabel grumbled.

'That's not good – poor you! Here – I made some smoothies of my own this morning. Have a try.' Rhanna pulled a jug of dark red juice from the fridge and poured three glasses. She handed one to each of the girls, and Isabel took a big swig.

'Mmm, that's lovely! Banana, strawberry… and something else?'

'It's honey and vanilla essence, together with a sprinkle of nutmeg. So what was the nightmare about, Elle?'

'Well – I don't really remember… ' Eleanor frowned. 'I keep getting tiny flashes of the dream – a storm; a garden… a journey. And I remember a man… ' she shook her head.

Rhanna put her smoothie down on the table.

'I wonder if your dream's trying to tell you something? I know that sounds stupid, but sometimes our minds try to work out problems for us when we are asleep, you know?'

'That's true, Rhanna,' Kelli said, overhearing her daughter as she came through from the shop. 'But this time, I think it's rather more than that.' She sat down at the table. 'I've left Emma in charge – things should be pretty quiet now the ladies from the course have settled. I think you need some help, yes?' Sipping her drink, Eleanor nodded.

'I had a dream – and then we found this in the dream catcher. We wanted to know what it was.' She rummaged in her bag and pulled out the hankie. She shook it and the broken ring dropped onto the table. Kelli looked at it closely.

'I don't know how this got to be in your dream catcher. I certainly didn't put it there – I've never seen it before.' She picked it up and turned it over in her hand.

'It looks really old.' She curled her fingers around the ring and closed her eyes. 'It has a lot of vibrations… some very dark . Whoah!' Her eyes flew open and she screwed up her face. 'It feels… wrong somehow. The surface feels greasy. Nasty thing!' She dropped it back on the table and prodded at it with a spoon handle. 'Would you mind if I borrowed it for a few days? I don't have any answers, but a friend of mine works at the Museum of Antiquities. I'll ask him to have a look, if that's OK with you.'

'Yeah – that's fine. I'm not really keen to take it home with me anyway.' Eleanor waved her hand in the air. 'When I touched it this morning, you'd think it had bitten me!' She made a high pitched, nervous noise that wasn't quite laughter. 'I even had to put on a plaster.' She slumped down into her seat as she looked at the ring. Kelli looked at her, her eyes narrowed and her head on one side.

'Interesting. We definitely need to know more. I have a few ideas, but I'd like to get them checked out before I share, OK?'

'That's great. Thanks Kelli.' Eleanor smiled. As they left the shop, she turned to Isabel. 'I think we should go down to St Andrews and have a look for ourselves. All in the name of research, of course!'

'Don't you think it's a bit ghoulish?' Isabel wrinkled her nose. 'Poking about in a graveyard? Especially one where bones keep surfacing – ugh!'

'Aren't you fascinated though? The idea that those bones have been hidden in the earth for over 350 years but are coming to the surface suddenly? Why now? There must be a reason.'

'Soil erosion? We learned about it when we were doing that geography project, remember? You know – where tonnes of materials blow away on the wind and get dropped somewhere else?'

'Yeah – but that was about the Gobi Desert – not some tiny churchyard in Newcastle! Anyway, it sounds like a really interesting church. It's really old.' She picked up a sheet of paper from the pile on the desk. 'It says here that there's a twelfth century lepers' squint... '

'Oh – charming!' Isabel frowned.

'No, listen – it's a special section built so people who were suffering from leprosy could still go to church and hear the sermons. People thought you'd go to hell if you didn't – they had to go every week. They might have got some comfort from the idea of heaven anyway, since their lives on earth were so horrible... anyway, they weren't allowed to mix with healthy people in case the disease spread. The people with leprosy could sit out of sight – and I bet people in the main church preferred that too because lepers could look really gruesome as the disease ate away at them…'

'Ew! Too much information!' Isabel clamped her hands over her ears.

'You must admit it would be interesting to see though…'

'Count me out. I think it's creepy.' Isabel shook her head. Eleanor pulled a sheaf of papers out of her bag and leafed through them.

'Hey – there's a bit here about the time just before the witches were buried at St Andrews. It says that during the civil war, Newcastle was a royalist stronghold – they supported the king. Anyway, when the Scots breached the city walls just by the church, lots of people were killed and St Andrews was half flattened! There had been a huge gun in the tower, so it had been fired on to hit the cannon. Amazing! It was so badly damaged that the church register says that they were no sermons or baptisms in the church for a whole year!'

'Hmmm… another cheerful story. Thanks for that.' Isabel grimaced.

'Aw, come on! It's interesting – you have to agree to that?'

'Well yes – in a sick, *Horrible Histories* kind of way I suppose.'

'Yeah – I can see it now: *Nasty Newcastle*!' Eleanor laughed. 'Come on, say you'll come with me and have a look… please?'

'Oh, all right. But don't expect me to like it. And no more grim stories!' Isabel wrinkled her nose.

'Great! No time like the present – let's go now.'

There were throngs of people coming from the cinema on Newgate Street and the road was busy. At the church gates, the girls entered another world.

'Wow! You wouldn't think we were still in the middle of town, would you?' Eleanor looked at an old graveyard full of moss covered stones. 'It's so… peaceful here.'

'You were expecting the inhabitants to be noisy?' Isabel made a ghastly face and wriggled her fingers in front of her.

'I mean, it feels… calm, somehow. Restful.' She wandered through the stones, pausing to read worn inscriptions.

'So many people died so young in the past, didn't they?' Isabel whispered sadly. 'I suppose healthcare wasn't as good then. Awful. So many little children.' She patted a gravestone as though to comfort herself.

'You know, we won't find stones for the witches.' Eleanor sighed. 'I remember reading on the Net that any prisoners hanged on the Town Moor were buried on the north side of the graveyard, in unconsecrated ground – you know, not blessed like this part. People used to believe that you wouldn't go to heaven if you were buried in unconsecrated ground.'

'Yeah – and they believed the world was flat, too!' Isabel frowned. 'But just because they didn't understand lots of stuff didn't mean they had to be cruel. Their relatives must have been so sad.'

'I know. Bad enough to lose someone you loved in such an awful way, but then to think you wouldn't see them in heaven – and that was all so many poor people had to look forward to, really – life was so grim. It makes me angry. And you know what made it even worse? Those silly, superstitious people thought the witches would *walk again* after death, like some stupid zombie film – so they put iron bolts into the knee joints of the executed people to stop them being able to walk!' Eleanor shook her head in disgust. 'Hey – look at this!' she called.

'I swear, if it's a bit of bone I shall throw up!' Isabel hissed.

'No – it's lovely. Come and see!' Eleanor had bobbed down and was brushing dry leaves away from a clump of small white flowers. 'Look – snowdrops. They're out of season, but aren't they lovely?'

Isabel heaved a sigh of relief. 'Very pretty. Global warming, I suppose – that's what always gets the blame for things happening out of season. Elle… ?'

Eleanor was cupping a petal with her fingers, staring into the centre of the flowers. Her mouth moved as though she was speaking, but Isabel could not hear what she was saying.

'Elle! Stop it – you're scaring me. That's not funny!' Isabel pulled at Eleanor's arm. 'Eleanor!' The girl's head moved slowly until she looked at her friend. When she began to speak, her voice was cracked and harsh.

'*They hanged us and brought us here – they pushed us in the earth as though to hide us. No pretty words; no mourners allowed. Later, in the darkness, Corvus dropped seeds from his beak onto the fresh soil. He marked my place with flowers – snowdrops, for the hope of life returning to the earth after the harshness of winter. Some say that in the language of flowers snowdrops mean the passing of sorrow.*'

'Elle… ?' Isabel whispered.

'*Yes, I am Ellenor.*' She nodded. '*But there was no resting place for any of us, thanks to the shape-shifter.*' She bared her teeth angrily as she spat the name. '*He is what many would call a demon.*' Her eyes widened suddenly. '*He comes!*' she cried, and then fell forwards, putting out a hand to save herself as she fell.

'Eleanor! What's the matter?' Isabel shouted.

'What? I said, look – snowdrops. Nothing's the matter. Then I lost my balance. Luckily I didn't squash them... what's up, Iz?' She stood and brushed off her jeans. Isabel stared at her with her mouth hanging open.

'But... y..you mean you weren't kidding about? So what was all that stuff about shape-shifters and being pushed in the earth?' Isabel stammered.

'Eh? What are you going on about, Iz? I was just admiring the flowers.'

'Something really creepy happened. You were looking right at me – but it felt like you were looking right *through* me. You spoke to me, but your voice sounded funny... not like you, really. And you were talking about what happened to the witches... as though you were one of them, Elle.'

Eleanor stared at Isabel. 'You aren't messing about, are you? You look scared. Hey – sorry, Iz – I didn't do it on purpose. Hell – I don't even remember it happening! This is beyond strange.' She put her hand to her forehead, and bent forwards. 'I feel really dizzy. Let's go home. I've lost all interest in looking round the church now. I think what we need to do is try to work out exactly what happened here. I'd really rather it didn't happen again!'

'You know, I hate to say this, but perhaps we should call in on Kelli again first and ask if she can help?' Isabel said, scraping her foot and making a bare circle in the soil. 'You were seriously strange there for a while, and it was to do with the witches... she's helped before, that's all. I just hope she doesn't get sick of us.'

'I can't see that happening. She's really into this. And I think we could both do with some of her *calming celestial tea*, or whatever she calls it,' Eleanor smiled shakily.

By the time they got back down to The Dancing Goddess, the door was locked. Eleanor rattled the handle.

'No problem – I'll ring Rhanna.'

'Or we could just knock on the door of the flat?' Isabel pointed at the gargoyle door knocker. Eleanor rubbed her face. 'Duh!'

Minutes later, they were sitting in Rhanna's bedroom. A *NightStalker* CD played in the background, and Rhanna pushed a pile of magazines off the bed.

'Sit down – sorry about the mess. Anyone want a drink?'

'Yeah – a juice would be great, thanks.' Isabel nodded.

As they sipped the cool drinks, Rhanna looked backwards and forwards between the two girls.

'Has something happened? You both look a bit... well, strange.'

'You could say that!' Isabel sighed. 'Something weird happened in the graveyard at St Andrews.'

'Sounds gothic,' Rhanna smiled. 'Do go on!'

'Well, one minute Elle was showing me some flowers; the next she was mumbling about shape-shifters and being hidden in the earth. And she said her name was Ellenor – like the witch we have been researching!' Isabel raised her eyebrows. 'Creepy, huh?'

'The worst thing is, I can't remember anything between pointing out the flowers and kind of falling forwards onto the dirt.' Eleanor frowned.

'I think that goes way past creepy into *bizarre* territory.' Rhanna shuddered. 'I guess you wanted my mum then, rather than me?'

'Well… we kind of wanted her slant on things, but we always like seeing you, of course.' Isabel patted Rhanna's arm.

'No worries. Actually, I have an idea about what happened.' Rhanna slid off the bed and typed something on her computer keyboard. She swung the screen round to face the girls.

'I think you might have been channelling your witch. She talks through you.'

'No way. No. That can't be right.' Isabel shook her head violently. 'it's just not possible.'

'Did it sound like Elle's voice?' Rhanna asked, consulting the screen again.

'Well… no. it was kind of raspy. But that might have been because she was cross.'

'And you have no memory of what you said?' Rhanna turned to Eleanor.

'Nope. None. I pointed at the flowers, then fell forwards. I can't remember the bit in the middle at all.'

'Did you feel kind of dizzy and weak afterwards?'

'I did, yes. I… I… hang on – I felt weird as soon as soon as I pointed at the flowers. I felt as though I was falling backwards without moving, if that makes sense?'

Rhanna nodded. 'Yeah – I think your witch must have been using you to communicate. What did you – she – say?'

'Well, I don't remember.' Eleanor shook her head and frowned. 'But Isabel said I was talking about the witches being buried in the churchyard, and then I warned us… ' she made a face as though she has tasted something bitter 'Sorry – this is just so confusing. It

makes me feel as though I don't know who I am any more.
Whoever it was doing the talking warned that we were in danger –
and that a *shape-shifter* was coming! It just sounds so stupid when
you say it out loud.' She shrugged.

'Well, I'm not an expert. Mum has a book here somewhere… '
Rhanna started searching a tall bookshelf. Her hand stroked along
the spines of the books as she passed them. 'Here it is!' She pulled
a slim paperback from the shelf. She leafed through the pages and
stopped to read.

'It says that this sort of channelling – where you haven't tried
to make it happen yourself, on purpose – is only likely to happen if
you have a strong connection to the person you are channelling,
and they have an important message to share. Well, we know that
there was an important message, if she was warning you about
danger from this shape-shifter, whoever that might be!' Rhanna
shut the book. 'Sorry my mum isn't here. She'd be a lot more help.'

'Actually, it helps to know you don't think I'm going mad!'
Eleanor smiled thinly. 'But I don't much like the idea that someone
else is talking through me, whoever that might be.'

Chapter Ten

T he next morning, Kelli swept into the Museum of Antiquities. She was carrying a small parcel wrapped in cloth. She waved her fingers at the receptionist.

'Hello Sue! Is Andrew there? He's expecting me – I spoke to him on the phone yesterday.' At that moment, a tall, slim man walked into the reception area.

'Kelli! Good to see you. I thought I'd wander down to see if you had arrived. If you don't mind, sign the visitors' book and come through. The coffee's on!' Kelli quickly signed her name and followed the man through to an office piled with books, papers, boxes and interesting looking artefacts.

'Sorry – bit of a mess. We are still getting organised!' He cleared a chair and invited Kelli to sit. He found two cups, and frowned at one of them. He blew into the cup hard and poked about inside with his finger. 'That one's mine then!' he said, pouring two steaming cups of coffee and offering one to Kelli. 'How's Rhanna? Well, I hope? Tell her to pop in and see me sometime soon – I'd love to hear her opinion on a new display I'm setting up for our Mithras exhibition. She loved the temple in the old museum, didn't she? Now, this all sounded intriguing on the phone. Is this the ring?' He pointed at the package Kelli had placed carefully on the desk.

'It is… I'd like you to have a look and see what you think.' She carefully unwrapped the ring, peeling back the wrappings without touching the cold metal.

'Oh – it doesn't look that delicate! Still – always better to be cautious with historic artefacts.' Andrew picked up the ring and turned it over in his hands. 'Hmm… Seventeenth century, I'd say. Strange… it feels oily somehow.' He rubbed his fingers together and looked at them, but could see no residue. 'A signet or *alliance* ring – showing membership of a group or guild… ' he nodded to himself. 'Where was it found?' Kelli shifted uncomfortably in her seat. Andrew was a scientist. How could she tell him a ghostly hand had placed it as a warning in a dream catcher?

'Erm… not sure. Locally. Friends of Rhanna's found it and wanted to know a bit more about it. Andrew – be careful with this ring. I think it has bad vibrations. Keep it wrapped in the protective coverings when you aren't examining it.'

Andrew looked at her, frowning. 'Bad vibrations?' He sighed. 'Kelli… '

'Just humour me, Andrew. Please?'

'OK. Leave it with me, and I'll see what I can find out for you. I'll write a few notes and will get the ring back to you in a few days.' Kelli stood, swigging the last of her still steaming coffee.

'Oh – are you in a hurry? I'd hoped we could have a bit of a catch up chat.' Andrew raised his eyebrows.

'Sorry, Andrew. Must dash – I have to get back to the shop. Why don't you call in for lunch when you have finished examining the ring? I could make you some of that lentil and potato soup you liked so much at the bring and share supper… ?'

'It's a deal! I'll give you a call once I've finished with the ring. Lovely to see you again.' He stood and followed Kelli as she walked back towards the reception area.

'Sorry I have to rush away. Thanks for this, Andrew.' She hugged her friend and waved, but as she left the building she felt the hairs stand up on the back of her neck. *Sorry Andrew*, she thought. *The truth is I can't bear to stay close to the malevolent aura given off by that ring, despite the protective bindings I have placed upon it.*

Back in the office, Andrew poked at the ring with a pencil as he finished the last of his coffee. *I don't like the way this feels... and I don't want to touch it again. Oh, Andrew – grow up. It's a ring. Kelli's your friend, but she can get a bit... over the top. It's just an old ring*, he thought to himself. He wiped his hands on a cloth, then thought better of it and went through to the sink in the lab. He squirted a dollop of pink soap and scrubbed hard, removing invisible dirt from his hands. *Get a grip!* He thought as he caught sight of himself in the mirror. As he was drying his hands, Beth walked into the room. She swished her long blonde hair out of her eyes.

'Hi Andrew! Anything interesting today? Been excavating a plague pit by any chance?'

Andrew looked at her, puzzled. 'Well – the way you were washing your hands. A bit extreme!'

'Hello to you too, Beth. Actually, a friend of mine just brought in a ring for me to look at. I think it's seventeenth century. I'll show you if you like.' He gestured into the office. 'How's life down at the Laing?'

'Great – always different, every day. Who wouldn't like working with those wonderful old pieces of artwork?' Beth worked deep in the basement of the Laing Art Gallery, restoring old and dirty paintings. 'Any coffee?' she asked hopefully.

'Help yourself. I've just had one thanks. Look – here it is.' He pushed the wrappings holding the ring towards her across the desk. Beth's eyes widened.

'Oh – wow – it can't be!' she squealed. 'No way! This is incredible!'

'Care to let me in on the amazing discovery?' Andrew peered at Beth over his glasses.

'I'm working on a portrait at the moment. It's really dark, even under the dirt. It's taking ages to clean because I'm having to go really slowly. It's a portrait of Kincaid, the witch finder from the seventeenth century. He was a busy boy in Scotland, from what I've read – he had thirty witches tried in Berwick, and then he came here to Newcastle to continue his disgusting work.' She glowered. 'Anyway, I've worked on his face – as you can imagine, he looks cruel and greedy. His eyes – they don't only *follow* you round the room – they bore into you! Yesterday I started cleaning the part of the portrait that showed his hands. That ring – it looks just like the one he was wearing in the painting! I can't be sure, but I'll take some photos if you don't mind… ' she scrabbled in her bag, pulling out a bus ticket, a half-empty bottle of water and a set of paint brushes. 'Aha! Here it is.' She produced her camera with a flourish and took several shots from different angles. 'Great! I'll print these off when I get back to the gallery and compare the two. How exciting. Watch this space! Thanks for the coffee. OK – I'll just grab the files I was after and I'll be off. See you soon.' In a flurry of papers she was gone.

'Um… bye to you too, Beth!' Andrew smiled at the door as it swung closed. He turned back to look at the cause of all the excitement. The ring had slipped off the wrapper and was lying on his desk. A dark shadow spilled from the ring, marking the desk like a stain. Andrew flipped it back on the wrapper with his pen. He tied the paper tightly, and locked the ring in his filing cabinet. He walked across to the heater and turned it up several notches. *It's getting cold in here...* he thought to himself. He ignored the quiet scratching noise he heard coming from the cabinet. He was a scientist, after all.

Chapter Eleven

The night was still and calm. Silver moonlight washed through the window, lapping across the foot of the bed. Eleanor was sleeping deeply. She kicked her legs as though she was trying to escape from something, but they tangled in her sheet.

Suddenly, she felt the air around her change. Her skirt was tangled round her legs and she stumbled. Ellenor walked with her head held high, looking straight ahead. The cold wind blew through the streets, stinging her cheeks and bringing with it the dank smell of the Tyne mud banks.

The crowd that had gathered along the road to watch the prisoners pass jostled for space, and rough voices shouted insults.

'Witch!'

'Dance with the devil? You'll dance at the end of a rope now!'

A gob of chewed tobacco landed on Ellenor's skirt. She looked up angrily into the face of the man wiping his mouth.

'Steady, Ben! She'll curse yer!' The man made a forked sign with his fingers, to cast aside the evil eye he feared, and then pushed backwards into the crowd. Ellenor scuffed her boot in the dirt, and walked on.

'Bless you, Mistress!' a quiet voice whispered urgently. She looked for the voice and saw Isabel, holding out a sprig of rosemary plucked from her own garden. She reached out, but was shoved sharply from behind. The rosemary fell from Isabel's hand as the crowd pushed together, and was crushed in the dirt. The crowd parted and a tall man stood waiting for the women. Ellenor saw a dark shadow, shimmering around the edges of the figure and her eyes widened. He stared at each woman in turn, his eyes burning them as he stared. The crowd fell silent.

'Good people of Newcastle!' the man called, raising his arms. 'I have been called here by the corporation to examine the wretches you see before you. I make a solemn promise to you now, that I shall root out the evil witches that have blighted your beautiful town.' He bowed his head.

'You do that, bonny lad!' an old woman shouted. 'They dried up my cows, they did – and they sent old Will mad with their shenanigans in the graveyard!' The crowd started to call out, jeering at the prisoners and shouting encouragement to the witch finder. He held up his hand and the crowd quietened.

'We shall examine them publicly. It worked in Berwick, where I found thirty of their number and it will work again here. I have my tools and will expose them for what they are.' He pulled a roll of brown leather from an inside pocket, and opened it with a flourish. He drew out a long, cruel point and waved it at the prisoners.

'Needles to prick the witch's marks I shall no doubt find upon you. The marks of Satan, placed upon your foul bodies by the Prince of Darkness, when you gave him your eternal souls. When I prick the marks and they do not bleed, you shall be exposed as the fiends I know you to be.' He circled the group of women as he spoke, and jabbed towards Ellenor with the needle. 'One we get you inside, we shall see *proof* of your evil craft!'

Ellenor's head snapped up. She glared at the witch finder, her eyes blazing.

'Satan? A pathetic invention, created to scare those who know no better. How can I sell my soul to a creature that does not exist? You sicken me. The stench of your evil chokes the air here.' She spat at the floor, and spittle spattered the man's black boots. He made a choked, disgusted noise in his throat, and pushed her towards the heavy oak door. She stumbled and was held up by the strong hand of a fat, middle aged man who nodded kindly as he released her arm.

'Careful, Mr Gardner… ' the witch finder growled. 'I am aware of your views, and have read some of your ridiculous testimonies. Be wary, lest they are mistaken for support for these wretches!'

Ralph Gardner stepped back and straightened his collar.

'I'll have you know that I am a well respected man in these parts. I'll thank you not to address me in this threatening manner, sir! And let me assure you that I shall be publishing full accounts of these proceedings – so let your treatment of these women be fair and just!'

'Oh, it will be *just*, do not fear… ' the witch finder sneered. He raised his arms again and roared to the crowd pressing in behind them. 'Justice will be meted out to these foul creatures and the blight of witchcraft will be banished from Newcastle!' The crowd cheered and pressed closer, their faces masks of hatred and fear. Ralph Gardner's face twisted with disgust. 'I shall be watching you, charlatan!' he muttered, as he pushed his way roughly through the crowd. Ellenor watched him go. She whispered 'Blessings be upon you, Ralph Gardner. May you stand as our witness down the ages, so those who follow us may know what happened here.'

'Enough, witch!' The witch finder grabbed Ellenor's arm, bruising the tender flesh with his fingers. 'You will spread your poison no longer!' He hissed, as he pushed Ellenor through the doorway. The prisoners were herded down a dark staircase and into a musty smelling cell. The door shut behind them with a clang.

'Make yourselves comfortable. You have a long stay ahead of you.' The witch finder purred as he leered through the bars in the door. 'But never fear – I shall try to get you out of here as soon as possible.'

'Thank you, sir.' A grey haired woman whispered. The witch finder smiled coldly at her, then mimed a noose tugging at his neck. He roared with laughter as her hand flew to her mouth and her eyes widened in horror. Ellenor bared her teeth at the man and flicked her fingers at him, before she put her arm around the woman's shoulder and led her away. The witch finder began to cough, and his eyes bulged as he struggled for air. He ran for the stairway and they heard him cursing and gasping as he leaned against the door at the top of the stairs.

'You will regret that, witch!' he rasped.

Ellenor felt the old woman tremble against her.

'Hush now mother. Do not let him see our fear. Come – we need to rest to keep our energy for the trials to come.' She squeezed the woman's shoulder and settled down with her on a patch of damp straw. 'This is not much of a bed, but we should try to sleep and gather our strength.' She listened to the scratching of rats in the darkness for a long time, until the old woman's quiet weeping stopped, and her breathing became even as she slept. Finally, Ellenor's eyelids drooped shut, and she dozed.

Ellenor dreamed that she was in her garden, the warm scent of apples tickling her nose. Skitterpaws rubbed round her legs. When her eyes opened she was confused, then remembered she was in the cell at the Castle Keep. Water trickled down the walls, and a sour smell rose from the pile of dirty straw under her. She tried to stand, but her legs buckled and she hit out at the wall with her hand to steady herself. Her knuckles scraped on the rough stone. She rubbed her gritty eyes with her fingers and looked around her. Women were slumped against the walls, and Ellenor could hear them groaning and weeping. A girl crouched on the floor, rocking backwards and forwards, muttering to herself. Ellenor stumbled across and knelt by the girl, laying her hand gently on her head.

'You are not alone, dear sister. Look into your heart and find a calm place to rest. Breathe deeply, and let the love of the Mother fill your soul with a warm glow.' The girl looked up at Ellenor, and her eyes focussed.

'Lady? I was alone in the dark… and then I heard your voice.' She grasped Ellenor's hand. 'Will we go home again, Lady? Will we feel the sun on our faces again?'

Ellenor stroked the girl's matted hair. 'I cannot make promises, my dear. But the mother holds us in her care and has a place for us all in her house, where we shall feel the sun on our faces for all eternity.'

The door of the cell smashed open, banging against the stone wall. A dark figure stood outlined against the light. Ellenor glared at the man as he came towards her.

'Stand, witch.' He growled. Ellenor forced herself upright. 'I ask you, Ellenor Henderson, are you ready to confess your sins and wash your stained soul clean?'

Ellenor curled her lip at the man. 'I have committed no sin, and the only blackened soul in here is yours, shape shifter,' she spat.

'Cease your lunatic ravings. I am Kincaid, summoned here to root out evil. But have it your way, woman. If you will not confess of your own free will, I shall enjoy… *encouraging* your tongue to loosen.' He grabbed Ellenor by the arm and dragged her towards the door. She struggled to stand. She was in a dark cell, lit only by a sputtering tallow candle. The witch finder loomed over Ellenor. His eyes gleamed as he poked her with his boot. She scowled, and his buckle caught in her ragged skirt. He grimaced, and pulled his foot free, tearing the wool.

'Enough of your tricks, wench!' he spat. 'I shall have a confession from you before long. I know your type… like all of your black-hearted sisters, you spread evil like seeds as you pass. I have variously heard that you only need to look at a cow for its milk to sour and curdle; that you travel across the county in spirit form, bewitching young men as they sleep. Some say you travel in the light of the full moon in a black spectral coach, pulled by *phookas*, their cloven hooves shod with fire that lights up the sky. I have heard tell that you brew noxious potions and spells to harm and hurt, and when we searched the hovel you call a cottage, we found evidence that damned you. Spell books; bunches of herbs gathered by the light of the moon, no doubt – and a pot of wax ready melted for making poppets to enslave the good people of this town. Some say you sail down the Tyne in a sieve on an All Hallows E'en, with the evil intent of sinking ships and drowning sailors as they cry for mercy. Witnesses say you consort with familiars shaped like a cat and a crow, which do your evil bidding. We shall root them out and destroy them, never fear.

Women like you, who traffic with the Prince of Darkness deserve to swing like the rotten fruit that they are on the gallows

tree… and my dear,' he caressed her flushed cheek with his black gloved hand, 'where you are concerned, I shall enjoy every moment of watching you twist at the end of a rope.' Ellenor turned her cheek and seemed to rest it against the arm richly clad in black velvet. The witch finder's eyes smouldered as he stared at the woman looking up at him. Like a snake striking, she sank her sharp little teeth into his wrist. He wrenched his arm from her grip, and crimson flowed across his cuff.

'Witch!' He drew back his hand and slapped her head so hard it struck the slimy wall of the cell, and she slid to the floor, unconscious.

Chapter Twelve

Eleanor woke with a gasp, and her hand flew to her cheek. She stared round the bedroom, wide eyed. She struggled to untangle herself from the bedding, and caught sight of herself in the mirror. A livid red mark streaked her face. She moved closer to the mirror and looked at her cheek. She traced the mark on her cheek with her fingers. It's a hand mark... she thought, and her heart lurched uncomfortably in her chest.

'Elle!... Eleanor! Time to get up. Breakfast's on the table.' Her mum's voice floated up the stairs. Eleanor took one last look in the mirror. She pulled on a sweatshirt and walked down the stairs. Her mum was standing at the cooker, frying little brown patties.

'Buckwheat and blueberry pancakes – I got the recipe from your Uncle Jay... but mine don't look like his. *They* were like delicious, sweet little clouds – and mine are more like concrete Frisbees!' She turned to scoop a pancake onto a plate and caught sight of Eleanor's face. She dropped the pancake onto the floor and the cats immediately ran across to sniff it.

'What have you done to your face?' she gasped.

'I'm fine, Mum – I think I must have been lying funny, or bashed myself in the night. This mark wasn't there when I went to bed.' She rubbed the red patch, and sent a dart of pain across her cheek.

'Here, take this clean cloth and hold it on your face.' She ran the tea towel under the cold tap, frowning. 'It looks sore.' She looked down and saw the cats tearing the pancake into pieces and batting them round the floor.

'Oh dear! Even Lila and Maverick won't eat my pancakes. Ah well... there's fruit and yoghurt in the fridge.' She cleared the squashed pancake into the bin. 'We'll have to keep an eye on that cheek, in case it's an allergic reaction to something. But we haven't been using different soap or anything...' she shook her head. 'Anyway, Isabel just rang. She says she'll be a bit late because she's picking up some papers on the way over, from Rhanna's house. I'm very glad to see how keen you are on this project! Right – I have to go and write my article; you keep that cloth on your face for a bit longer and I'll look at it again later.'

By the time Isabel knocked at the door, the redness on her cheek was fading. On the way to let her in, Eleanor looked in the mirror on the hall stand and moved her jaw experimentally. She prodded her cheek and winced. *I'm going to have a bruise...* she frowned. She opened the door, and Isabel rushed in, waving a folder.

'Wait 'til you see this!' she slipped off her jacket and hung it on the stand. She turned towards Eleanor. 'Hey – what's wrong with your face?'

Eleanor pursed her lips. 'Well, I don't really know. I woke up with a red mark, as though I'd been slapped really hard. You know that time the swing doors at the swimming pool smacked me in the face and I chipped my tooth? It felt like that. But I'd only been in bed, so that doesn't make sense. My mum flipped when she saw it – she had me sat there with a cold compress! The strange thing is, as I sat here holding it on my face, I kept having funny thoughts – flashes of pictures like stills from a film, but they came from my dream. I saw this woman with long red hair being slapped by a tall man in black – on the same cheek as where my mark appeared.' She bent her head forwards and hid her face in a curtain of hair. 'I think I'm going crazy.'

'You poor thing! Is your face still sore?' Isabel's brows knitted together.

'Much better than it was – but I think I'm going to have a bruise. But how can a dream hurt you like this?'

'Well, if you think about it, your bad dream could have made you thrash about and hit yourself accidentally. Or, you could have bashed yourself and your mind could have created the slap in the dream to match it. There's always a logical explanation. Except… '

'What?'

'Well, Rhanna told me that Kelli's friend got very excited when he saw the ring. I've got some notes about it here. Apparently, it's a rich man's signet from the seventeenth century. OK, so far, so good. But here's the weird part. There's a huge portrait in the storage area at the Laing Art Gallery, in Newcastle, of this scary looking man. Well, one of the women doing the restoration on the portrait also works on artefacts at the museum of Antiquities. She saw the ring when Kelli's friend was examining it – and she recognised it. From the portrait she was working on, I mean.'

Isabel pulled a print of the portrait out of the file and handed it to Eleanor. A brooding man with eyes as dark as beetle wings stared back at her. Her cheek began to throb.

'You can't see it in great detail here, but look – here's a close up.' Isabel pushed another picture into Eleanor's hand. It was the ring with the same crossed keys design, but in the picture it was shining and new. 'And that's not all.'

Eleanor's hand was shaking so hard that the paper she held flapped like a fan. The colour had drained from her face.

'He's the witch finder, isn't he?' she asked in a quiet voice.

'Well – yeah. I thought I was bringing *big* news. They think the portrait may be Kincaid, the witch finder. How do you know? Have you seen the picture before?'

'No. But I know that man, Izzy.' Eleanor whispered. 'The man in the picture – he was the one in the dream – the one who slapped the woman!'

Isabel sat down hard on the bed. 'Now wait a minute. Let me think… there has to be an explanation here – I know! You must have seen the portrait before.'

'But you said the painting was in storage.'

'Well, OK – perhaps you saw the picture reproduced in one of those creepy old books from the Lit and Phil.'

'I don't remember seeing it, but I guess it's possible. But that still leaves something that can't be explained though. How did *his* ring – a ring that Kelli had never seen before – appear in my bedroom, caught in the dream catcher? Give me a logical explanation for that, Izzy!'

Isabel pursed her lips and frowned. 'I can't explain it, Elle. And if I could, I don't think you'd listen.' She fiddled with a tissue, tearing it into tiny pieces. 'Anyway, Kelli has your ring back now.'

'It's OK, Iz.' Eleanor sighed. 'I know I sound mad. But I've had an idea that might help to clear up some of this confusion. Will you come with me to the Castle Keep? Maybe it won't look like the place in my dream, and then I'll know I'm imagining some of this stuff. We can always call in at the library later. And you could take some really great photos for the project… ' Eleanor wheedled. 'Atmospheric and gothic – they'd be great for your portfolio. I just need to check out the details from my dream.' She shivered.

'OK… I'm sold.' Isabel smiled. Let me get my stuff together – I'm presuming you want to go today, Miss *Eager*? You know – it won't be anything like your dream. It's worth going, just to prove *that*, and stop you from worrying.'

'Yeah – I'd like to go now if you don't mind. You know me so well. Tell you what – I'll nip downstairs and see what I can scrounge from the fridge in the way of a picnic and then we'll be set.'

An hour later they were standing in front of the Keep. Eleanor walked ahead, up the sandstone staircase.

'Look at these steps, Izzy – they're worn in the middle where so many feet have walked up them over the centuries! It's kind of sad to think the witches would have been here too.'

'Yeah – it's quite something. Actually, I was thinking how hard it would be to walk up all these steps wearing a long, heavy dress – you'd be shattered!' Isabel took a close up picture of the castle steps, showing the detail of the tread of long-ago feet.

The girls paid at the kiosk and walked inside.

'Well – so far, so good – it doesn't look anything like my dream.' Eleanor peered around her. They looked at historical artefacts in carefully lit cases.

'It's incredible to think there's been a castle here for a thousand years! And a Roman fort before then – amazing. And I can just imagine the Royalists defending the castle during the Civil War.'

'So can I – I bet they had those lovely big hats with feathers on too – very dashing!' Eleanor pretended to fight with a sword, weaving and bobbing around Isabel.

'Come on then – let's go and have a look round. I want to see if any of the things I saw in my dream are the same here.'

'I'm sure they won't be – don't worry!' Isabel pushed her hair out of her eyes. 'Come on – let's go to the Great Hall first.' The girls followed the signs, and Eleanor traced her fingers across the rough sandstone walls as she walked. She snatched her hand back as she remembered the same feeling from her nightmare. The corridor opened into the Great Hall, and Eleanor let out a deep breath.

'Iz – it's not the room from my dream! Well – it looks a bit like it, but the ceiling's all wrong, for a start – it's much too high, and it's made of stone. The ceiling of the room in my dream was made of wood. It was low, and thick smoke from the fireplace gathered under the ceiling in thick clouds and filled the room. And that window wasn't there!' she pointed.

'Told you!' Isabel nodded smugly.

'Well, since we're here, let's have a look at the displays. And I want to have a look in this 'Queen's Chamber,' just down those stairs. She trotted down the stairs leaving Isabel reading a display board. As she went round the corner, she squealed. A woman stood in the Queen's Chamber, staring at her. 'Izzy! Oh… !' Isabel rushed into the room, banging into Eleanor.

'What is it? I heard you – oh.' Isabel gasped. 'I wasn't expecting that!' The Queen's chamber was set up with a display of how the room may have looked when it was used, complete with mannequins.

'I thought… ' Eleanor blushed.

'I know.' Isabel patted her friend's shoulder. 'But it's just a model.'

'Tell you what – on the way down here I saw a great stone pier supporting the roof – that wasn't here in my dream either. I don't know why I'm being so jumpy.'

Isabel pursed her lips. 'Well… there is something you need to know. I was reading those boards upstairs – so I could show off when I got home, really and blind the family with my brilliance – and it says that the roof in the Great Hall wasn't always that high. And there wasn't a window – the room used to be lower, before they restored it in the 1800s. And that pier you were talking about? Added much later to make the place safe.'

The colour ran from Eleanor's face. 'So you mean… ?'

'All I mean is that it didn't always look this way. That doesn't mean your dreams were what really happened. You could have read about it and forgotten. You've always had a great imagination. Look at the stories you write. Don't let it get to you.'

Eleanor sat down hard on the floor. 'Thanks, Iz – but I don't think that's it.' She sighed. 'Come on then – let's check out the rest of this place.' Isabel pulled Eleanor to her feet.

'Elle, I think we should give the next room a miss! According to the board upstairs, it's called *the bloodstained chamber*. Shall we check out the roof instead?'

'Sorry, Izzy… there's something I need to look at in there. In my dream, there was a small room where the witches were questioned. And the witch finder… he hurt them, Iz. Ellenor was questioned in there, in my dream. She bit him, and he hit her hard. She fell against the wall and bashed her head, and it made her bleed. I remember seeing the bloodstain on the wall. I need to see if it's really there.'

'But Elle – sorry, but that's daft! We're talking about over three hundred and fifty years ago! Even if what you saw in your dream was real – which I doubt – the stain wouldn't still be there!' Isabel frowned.

'OK – but I need to look. Will you come with me?' Eleanor asked, resting her hand on her friend's arm.

'Come on then – for what it's worth!' The girls walked slowly to the north corner of the Great Hall.

'Are you ready for this? It's supposed to be up these stairs.' Eleanor whispered.

'Go on, then!' Isabel nudged her towards the steps. Resting her hand on the rough wall, Eleanor started to climb. As she entered the chamber she felt the air press hard against her.

'It happened there… in the corner of the room. He slapped her and her head hit the wall. It should be opposite where we are standing, by the window.' She walked slowly towards the corner of the room.

'Elle! What's that?' Isabel hissed. She was pointing at a dark red stain on the wall.

'I… I guess it could be some sort of iron stain? You know like we saw in those rocks when we went on the trip to the moors?' Isabel whispered. Eleanor reached out and touched the stain with her fingers. A strange prickling sensation shot through her hand

and up her arm.

'But Iz – the stain's in the mortar between the stones too. This stain is from something being splashed against the wall. I think… I think it was Ellenor's blood!'

The room filled with a sighing noise. Wind suddenly whipped around the girls, flicking their hair and rustling the leaflets sticking out of Eleanor's bag. Eleanor felt something brush her cheek. A gentle hand stroked her face and a voice murmured in her ear.

'Do not mourn for me. I was imprisoned here. The custodian today is a good man who prays for our souls. But you must leave now. The shape-shifter's evil is strong here – the demon's darkness permeates the very walls.'

'Did you hear that?' Eleanor whispered. She shook her head as though she needed to clear it. 'No… no, I don't suppose you did.'

'What is it, Elle? I heard the wind – hell, I *saw* the wind. Everything was blowing about. Do you think someone left a window open somewhere?'

'I heard her voice, Iz – Ellenor's voice. She says it's her blood on the wall. But we have to hurry – she was warning us to get away from here. She says the witch finder's evil is very strong here and we're in danger!'

'Oh, come on Elle – you're just imagining things because this place is so gloomy.'

Eleanor grabbed Isabel's arm and tugged her towards the stairs. Her eyes were wide. A scraping noise came from above them, and the sound of heavy footsteps.

'OK – let's go!' Isabel hissed. They clattered down the stairs towards the entrance. A man suddenly filled the doorway in front of them, making a dark shape against the bright sunlight outside.

'Elle!' Isabel shrieked. The man reached a hand towards them. 'It's him!' the girls grabbed hold of each other and backed into the wall. A man stepped forward into the light.

'Steady on girls – please don't run down the stairs. You might slip, and hurt yourselves!' It was the Keep custodian. As he stepped towards the girls, they glanced at each other and began to laugh. He smiled, uncertainly.

'When you were coming down those stairs you looked like the hounds of hell were after you! Surely it's not that bad? Or did you see one of our ghosts? We have a few, you know. I suppose it's not surprising considering the long and bloody history of this place. They even hold ghost investigations here, you know! Have you seen the mark of the blood on the wall in the blood stained chamber? I thought I could hear you up there. Nobody knows what happened there, or who the unfortunate victim was.' The girls exchanged a glance. Isabel raised her eyebrows.

'There are lots of theories. I think it must have been a woman though. Sometimes, when I'm here by myself locking up I think I can hear a poor soul crying. I've even heard a woman singing softly to herself sometimes. But when I go in there, there's no one there. I've said some prayers for her though. It makes me feel so sad to think she was so unhappy.'

'She's very gratef… I mean, I'm sure she's very grateful. I think that's really nice of you.' Eleanor smiled. The custodian looked puzzled.

'OK… anyway – be careful, girls. You could really get hurt on those stairs. Make sure you have a walk around outside. And go and look at The Black Gate if you get a chance – it's really interesting!' He went back to his kiosk and opened the door. 'Do come again – but remember, no running!'

'Thanks! We will. Bye!' The girls walked quickly down the stairs, back into the street.

'That was scary!' Isabel shook her head. 'Of course, we mainly managed to scare ourselves... but... .' She looked over her shoulder at the Keep. 'I've got a horrible prickly feeling in the back of my neck, like we were being watched, you know?'

'Oh, I do. This place is really creepy!' Eleanor rubbed the back of her neck and shook her hair. 'Come on, let's go and have our picnic. We can sit on the wall there in the sun. Let's leave The Black Gate until this afternoon.' As the girls walked away from the keep, a dark shadow watched them from the narrow window.

'I was close this time. You may have escaped me today, but you cannot escape me forever. You will be mine!' a cold voice hissed.

Downstairs, the custodian looked up into the gloom. He rubbed his hands together and blew on them. *It's getting cold in here*, he thought. Then he backed away from the stairs, still staring up into the darkness. Feeling his way to the the kiosk, he hurried inside and locked the door tight. He turned the radio up loud, and tried hard to concentrate on reading his new book.

Chapter Thirteen

After lunch, Eleanor collected the rubbish together and drop kicked it into the bin. 'And she scores… and the supporters go wild… ' she cupped her hands and made the noise of a roaring, cheering crowd. Isabel clapped slowly, and wrapped up a leftover sandwich.

'I'm stuffed. I thought you were just grabbing a few things? There was enough there to feed a football team! Still, I feel better now. I think we just spooked ourselves this morning because of your dream.'

Eleanor bit her lip.

'That's just it. So much there was from my dream. It was more like a memory.'

'I'm sure we'll find a rational explanation, Elle – don't let it get to you.'

The girls walked down to The Black Gate. Isabel rummaged in her bag for her camera.

'OK – so far, so good! This place isn't creepy – it's just old! Stand there, Elle – let me take a photo.' She pointed at the arch. 'That frames the sunlight really well – what a shot!' Isabel fussed Eleanor into position then started taking pictures.

'These are going to be great! Now, I know you're itching to do it. Break open the guide books!' Eleanor tugged a book out of her back pack.

'Well, it says here that the gate was the last part of the castle's defences. It used to have drawbridges where these wooden footbridges are today.' Eleanor stamped her foot on the wood and a hollow sound echoed round the gateway.

'Maybe it is spooky after all!' Isabel ducked as a crow sheltering under the archway squawked noisily into flight.

'Anyway, it was first built in 1247 but added to in the seventeenth century. And this is interesting... it didn't get its name because it looks spooky and gothic – it got its name from Patrick Black, a merchant who lived here with his wife! And there were houses built here in the seventeenth century, too. It must have looked so different when our witches were imprisoned here... Hey – in 1636 it was a pub! Can you believe that? A man called John Pickles was the landlord. It says in the book that you can see his name scratched into the stone on the south west wall. That would be... ' she walked towards the wall 'here! Look! Seventeenth century graffiti! Amazing!'

'That is pretty interesting, Elle. If we scratched our names, it would be vandalism – but he did it and it's history!' She shook her head theatrically.

'Hey look – that crow's come back.' Eleanor pointed. 'Take some pictures of it, Izzy. They'll help you with your sketches – or you could be really arty and display them together!' Isabel framed the crow under the arch of the bridge.

'That'll make a good shot.' The crow hopped nearer to the girls. 'Hey – have you got any of that sandwich left? If you have, throw it on the grass so he comes over here. I'd like to get a shot in front of the wall there – very atmospheric!' Eleanor rustled in the bag, and the crow hopped closer.

'It's working... throw some over here.' Isabel whispered. She carried on taking pictures as the crow hopped towards them and pecked at the crusts. As it opened its beak, something glittered in the sunlight and fell onto the grass.

'Hey – it dropped something!' Eleanor shouted. The bird burst into flight with a beating of strong black wings. A glossy black feather fluttered to the ground, whirling in circles like a sycamore key as it fell. Eleanor rushed forwards and picked it up.

'Thanks for that!' Isabel grumbled. 'Why did you yell? I was getting some great pictures there!'

'Sorry! But did you see something fall too?' Eleanor scanned the grass.

'Well, yeah – a feather, but you've picked that up already.'

'No… something shiny fell from its beak as it went for the bread.'

'Elle – it's a carrion crow, not a magpie!' Isabel put her camera carefully in its bag. Eleanor got down and started crawling around on the grass, running her fingers through the tufts.

'I saw something, Iz.' The crow circled overhead, cawing at the girls.

'Hey – if you did, I think he wants it back!' Isabel laughed. The crow flew lower, and started to dive-bomb a clump of long grass.

'Actually, I think he's trying to show me where it is!' Eleanor shouted. She scurried across and began to sift through the grass. The crow rose higher, but continued to circle. Eleanor's fingers closed round something cold and smooth. She pulled her hand out of the grass.

'Wow! Izzy, look at this!' She held out a heavy silver pendant, studded with gems. 'This looks like it's worth something! Look –

it's got a pearl set into it. And that stone at the top looks a bit like my mum's citrine ring.' She turned it over in her hand. 'You're not going to believe this.' The back of the pendant was engraved with old fashioned writing.

Ellenor Henderson, 1642

'No way. It must have been Ellenor's! It's got her name engraved on the back. The crow was trying to show us something. Thanks, crow! Or should I say Corvus?' She heard cawing and looked up. A soft downy feather fluttered down from the sky, but the crow had disappeared.

'Let me see.' Isabel held out her hand. She took the pendant and turned it over slowly in her hand. 'I don't believe this. This *cannot* be happening. Elle, this is just getting freaky. Perhaps this time we're both dreaming?' She rubbed her eyes, then handed back the pendant.

'I'd offer to pinch you, but you might complain.' Eleanor shrugged. 'Welcome to my world.'

'But… how could this happen?'

'You tell me. I'd love to have one of your rational explanations, Iz – but I just don't think there is one. Not this time. This pendant is real. It has her name on it.' She slumped down onto the grass and stared at the necklace. Isabel sat down next to her.

'Elle – I think we're really getting out of our depth here. Do you think we should talk to our parents about it all? They might come up with some sort of explanation.'

'Iz – think about it. Can you imagine trying to explain even a tiny part of this? They'd think we were making it up as a joke, or that we were watching too many scary films – and that's the best case scenario. At worst, they could think we were going all *Marilyn Manson* on them and we could find ourselves never allowed out of the house again – think about it. I think we need to deal with this ourselves.' She rubbed her hand over her face. 'Well – at least we have Kelli to help us too.'

'Oh – great.' Isabel grimaced. 'That makes me feel so much better. *Glenda the Good Witch* is on the case. ' She held up her hand. 'No, I know, she's lovely – but she's just too into all this weird stuff to step back and think about it logically.' Eleanor leaned forwards and took hold of Isabel's arm. 'That's where you come in, Izzy. The voice of reason.'

'Yeah – but that didn't stop me squealing and running away from the custodian at the Keep, did it? OK – we'll try and sort this out ourselves. You win – for now. Come on, it's getting late. We can go to the library another day. I've had enough. Let's go home.'

Back at Isabel's house that evening, the girls sat in front of the computer. A woodcut of four witches hanging from a wooden gallows filled the screen. Eleanor bit her lip.

'Izzy – this is the picture I was talking about. From the book at the Lit and Phil – look at the label on the picture.'

This illustration is taken from Ralph Gardner's England's Grievance Discovered in Relation to the Coal-Trade 1655.

'Yeah? So?' Isabel opened her bottle of lemonade with a hiss.

'Ralph Gardner.' Eleanor raised her eyebrows and nodded.

'Who?' Isabel slurped the fizzy drink.

'Remember, he was in my dream – the man who helped me… '
she shook her head. 'Who helped Ellenor when she stumbled? The
man who said he'd write about what happened? Izzy – I think that
somehow I saw into the past. I saw what happened to the witches
as though I was there. My dreams are like films replaying in my
head. They are so vivid – I can see things… hear and smell
things… and even feel things.' She closed her eyes. 'I think these
things really happened. I keep finding proof, like this picture. And
don't tell me that I must have read about Ralph Gardner before – I
haven't!'

'Did I say a word?' Isabel asked. 'Listen, Elle – I don't think…
hang on, what was that?' Something was tapping against the
window. 'A tree branch, yeah?' she looked at the window, wide
eyed.

'Except there's no tree there – I bet it's Luke messing about!'
Eleanor stalked across the room to the window. As she peered out
into the night, her own face stared back, mirrored by the darkness
of the window. The tapping continued. Eleanor jumped back
suddenly.

'Izzy… ?'

Tap. A luminous white moth banged against the glass. Tap.
Another moth crashed into the window, battering its furry head
against the cold surface. Tap, tap, tap. More moths pressed against
the glass. Eleanor looked down. The window sill was covered in
small fluffy bodies, antennae flicking and wings pattering against
the window. As more taps sounded, silky bodies piled up against
the glass.

'Izzy – turn the light off! It must be attracting the poor things!'
Isabel shot across the room and hit the switch, plunging them into

darkness. The only light was the green glow from the computer screen. Isabel looked as though she was swimming underwater as she felt her way back across the room to the window.

'What on earth is going on here... ?' Isabel whispered. The girls stared into the darkness as the moths crawled across the window, leaving shimmering dust from their wings on the glass. Suddenly, as though they had received a signal, they fluttered of into the night.

'Ugh! Creepy crawlies! 'I *hate* creepy crawlies.! I'm going down to get a snack. Maybe some crisps to go with this drink?' Isabel ran down the stairs.

'That was... weird.' Eleanor whispered. 'And that's just not possible.' Writing was appearing on the glass, scratched into the glittery dust.

Help us

'Look! Izzy, come and look at this!' Eleanor called down the stairs. 'Come quickly!'

Isabel ran up the stairs clutching a family bag of crisps and an empty bowl. 'What's the matter? What's going on?' She ran into the bedroom, her eyes raking the room. Eleanor pointed at the window. The writing had gone.

'There was... ' she shook her head. 'Never mind. Sorry Iz. I thought I saw something, but I must have made a mistake.' She rubbed her hand across her eyes. Isabel frowned. 'I thought something was wrong.' She tore the bag open and tipped the crisps into the bowl. 'What did you think you saw? It must have been quite something.'

'Nothing. I… I think I'm just… tired. Sorry Iz. Can we just forget about it?'

'OK Elle. But I think those moths were weird enough without imagining anything else.'

Eleanor's head whipped up. 'I didn't imagine anything. I just made a mistake, that's all. Anyway, I'd better go. It's getting late.'

'Elle… ' Isabel grabbed her friend's arm. 'I didn't mean *anything*.'

Eleanor pursed her lips. 'I know. It's OK. I just have to get home. You know what my Mum's like if I'm late. I'll see you tomorrow. Don't forget, we're meeting in Leazes Park at lunchtime.'

'If you're sure you're OK… hey! My dad could give you a lift home.'

'Do you think he'd mind?' Eleanor stared out into the darkness.

'I'm sure he'll offer as soon as we get downstairs. Just you wait!' As the girls came downstairs, Mr Price was pulling on his coat.

'That's good timing! I just spoke to your mum, Elle. I said I was on my way to collect those windfall plums from her that she promised me for my jam making, and I'd drop you off at the same time. That OK with you? It's a wild, windy night out there.'

'Told you!' Isabel whispered. 'I'll come too for the ride, Dad.' She pulled on her coat. Outside, the wind tugged at their hair and snatched the car door out of Isabel's hand.

'Careful, Iz!' her Dad grimaced as the metal made a sickly

grinding sound.

'It wasn't my fault, Dad! The wind tried to turn the car inside out!'

'Odd, isn't it? It was such a still night earlier. Your Mum and I were watching the last hawk moths of the season as they fluttered round the light in the garden. There were loads of them, and even a few bats chasing them.'

Eleanor and Isabel glanced at each other.

'We saw a lot of moths earlier, too.' Eleanor swallowed hard at the memory.

'And now these high winds. It's cold suddenly, too.' Mr Price turned up the heater in the car. Outside, the darkness pressed against the windows. Isabel reached out and pressed the central locking button. Her dad glanced at her, and then turned on the CD player.

'*I need a bell, book and candle, to keep your ghost away…*' he sang along with the music, tapping his fingers on the steering wheel. 'You can't beat a bit of Boo Hewerdine. Better than those groups of yours, girls!' he teased.

'I think that's what we need tonight – an exorcism!' Eleanor whispered in her friend's ear. Isabel pushed her away.

'Don't! It's not funny!' she hissed, her eyes wide in the darkness. Her dad hummed on, oblivious of the commotion in the back.

'I was just kidding, Iz. Sorry…' Eleanor turned to look out of the window. The wind threw rubbish past them, and it picked up a traffic cone and threw it across the road. Mr Price swerved to avoid it.

'Hey – I'm glad you didn't get the bus home in this, Elle!'

'You and me both, Mr Price! I'm very grateful.'

'Not a problem. And I get those free plums from your mum's freezer into the bargain!'

As they pulled into the driveway at Eleanor's house, dark shadows poured across the garden. The trees whipped in the wind, scraping bony fingers against the fence. Neither girl moved.

'Come on Eleanor!' called Mr Price as he bounded from the car and up the steps. He knocked on the door and Eleanor's mum opened it, bathing the yard in light.

'You're not leaving me out here alone!' Isabel leaped out of the car, and the girls rushed into the house. As she closed the door behind her, Eleanor couldn't stop herself from staring out into the night one more time. It felt as though something in the darkness stared back.

Chapter Fifteen

The next morning was bright and the sun warmed Eleanor's face as she carried her sandwich bag into the park and sat by the pond. The sun glinted on the surface of the water, and an electric blue dragonfly flitted from plant to plant, snatching midges from the clouds of insects that still drifted across the pool. *Last night, it was moths and bats… today, a dragonfly. Is it global warming, or is the summer following me? Don't these creatures know it's November?* Eleanor puzzled. As she ate, she stared into the water, watching tiny transparent fish slipping through blankets of weed. She finished her sandwich and dangled her fingers in the water. A pond skater skidded across her reflection. Suddenly, Ellenor's face looked back at her from the water. Eleanor jumped as a voice sounded in her head.

'I must be swift. You have found my treasures yet there are things I still need you to find. You have experienced the shape-shifter's darkness. He holds my soul, and the souls of my sisters in his power. As we died – as a result of his evil – he trapped our souls in poppets. Dark dolls he fashioned for his purpose, with strands of our hair and shards of our nails. He did this to harness our powers, to use them for his own ends. I managed to weave a spell that tempered his magick – he could not force our souls to do his will, as he wished, unless he held the pendulum of power. I knew that I had hidden the crystal, and that he would not find it. Now you hold the pendulum and he senses that it is active once

again. He is drawn to it like a dark insect to a flame.'

Her image flickered as the surface of the water rippled.

'Beware, Eleanor. He will stop at nothing to gain power. He hungers for the freedom the pendulum offers him, and will hunt you like a ravenous wolf. Yet I would still ask you to help us. You are young, but you have deep inner strength. I see your power thrumming through you. The demon will see it too, and crave it for himself.'

She held out her hand towards Eleanor, and their fingers touched on the cold surface of the water.

'Eleanor, I shall protect you in every way I can. But what I ask of you now is perilous. You must find the poppets that bind us and destroy them with fire. That will release our souls so we may travel on to the Summerlands. At present, we are lost in the mists. You and I are bound together by the power of the pendulum, so I may contact you. But many here with me are lonely. They ache with the need for peace. They wander restlessly, pulling at their hair and tearing their garments in their sorrow. You have the power to end this torment. You must use the pendulum to find the poppets. Hold the crystal above a map of the town. They must be nearby, as he needs to keep them close to our bones for the binding spell to work. Keep a picture of the poppets in your thoughts, and focus on your will to find them. The pendulum will turn in circles, and will pull towards the area you need to search.'

Dark mist began to uncoil behind Ellenor's face.

'I must go… he draws near, seeking me.'

The surface of the pool darkened, and soon the only movement

Eleanor could see were fronds of pond weed wafting backwards and forwards in the deep green water.

'Hi Elle! Sorry I'm late!' Isabel flopped down on the grass and pulled a plastic box out of her bag. 'Pasta salad? My Mum made it this morning. Or would you prefer a cheese roll? Mum went a bit overboard. Did your Mum find what she wanted at the library?'

Eleanor turned her face towards Isabel, but she had a faraway look in her eyes. 'Oh – hi Iz. Did you have a good time this morning?'

'At the Dental Hospital? Hardly. There's a chance I might need a brace. Actually, the ones they showed me didn't look too bad. They had some nice colours. Elle? Are you listening to me at all?' Eleanor was staring at the pond.

'Hmm? Yes. A brace. OK.' Eleanor looked at her friend. 'Sorry Izzy. I've just been thinking about stuff, that's all. Look – there's a dragonfly, in November!'

'Don't tell me what you've been thinking about. If it has to do with witches I think I'll scream.' Isabel frowned.

Eleanor winced. 'Get ready to yell then. I just saw… something that I need to tell you about.'

'Apart from a dragonfly that shouldn't be flying around on a strangely warm November day. I'll give you that it's weird, but it's hardly supernatural.'

'I saw Ellenor again.'

'Where?' Isabel spun round, looking across the park.

'In the pond. Well, sort of.' She held up her hand as Isabel opened her mouth to speak. 'No, listen for a minute. I know what I'm saying sounds stupid. I was looking into the pond, watching the water boatmen, and wondering why there were summer bugs here that should be long gone. Then her face appeared. She spoke to me, Izzy! Well, I heard her voice in my head. She told me about a man… a demon… she called the *shape-shifter*. She said he had trapped the souls of the people hanged as witches on the Town Moor so he could have their power for himself. She said they were trapped because of the poppets he made. They're like dolls. Izzy, she wants us to find them so those poor souls can be set free.'

Isabel stared at Eleanor, holding a cheese roll half way to her lips. Her mouth hung open.

'Are you serious? You thought you saw… heard that? You aren't kidding me?'

'No joke. She said the pendulum we found is very powerful, and we can use it to find the poppets.'

'Whew! Elle… are you sure? I mean… I believe you and everything, but that's a lot to take in.' Isabel shook her head.

'All we need is a map. Then we hold the pendulum over it and it will lead us to the poppets!' Eleanor's eyes shone.

'I don't know, Elle. It all sounds a bit weird. Listen to yourself. "*A witch spoke to me from a pond and now I need to use a magic crystal to find some nasty dolls…*" '

'Izzy! I know it sounds strange, but I'm serious. Please don't make fun of me.'

'Elle, I'm not trying to be horrible. But just think about what you're saying for a minute.' She sighed. 'I know I was scared last night. And I know that truly freaky things keep happening. Listen, if this is something you really want to do, you know I'll help you. But I don't have to believe it all and I certainly don't have to like it.

It scares me to hear you talk like this. You don't sound like… yourself.'

'Sorry, Iz. But this is something I… we… have to do. You should have heard her. They need our help. She sounded desperate.' She grabbed Isabel's hand. 'Come on – we can get a map from the library.'

Chapter Sixteen

That afternoon, back at home, Eleanor held the pendulum above the map of the city. The stone glimmered, casting flickers of underwater light on the paper. Eleanor looked at Isabel.

'So, I'm holding a picture of one of those horrible dolls in my mind – and I'd rather not! I think they're spooky. But to be honest, I feel a bit silly doing this. I can't see how it would work... oh!' The pendulum began to move, turning in tiny circles.

'Tell me *you're* doing that, right?' Isabel frowned. Eleanor shook her head. The pendulum began to move faster, swinging in wide circles across the map.

'I can feel it... sort of *pulling* at my hand!' Eleanor said breathlessly. The pendulum swung harder, tugging Eleanor's fingers towards the section of the map showing the Ouseburn Valley. The circles got smaller as the pendulum swung faster.

'Is it pointing at Seven Stories? The place we went with mum to see the book exhibition?' Isabel peered at the map. 'Elle... I just had a thought. What happens if there's a building on top of the poppets?'

'No... it's not Seven Stories... but it's definitely near the river there. Izzy, don't try and think of *more* problems – we'll face them if and when they appear.' Eleanor frowned. 'Hey! I think the pendulum is showing Ouseburn Farm. Look!' The pendulum quivered above the farm icon. The girls looked at each other. 'I

Town Moor

Haymarket
Bus Station

Northumbria
University

Eldon Square

City Library

St Andrew's
Church

Seven
Stories

Arts Centre

The Sage

Central Station

Castle Keep

Lit and Phil Library

think it's time for another trip into town!'

'OK – but you don't have to sound so happy about it!' Isabel huffed. Stuffing the map into her backpack, Eleanor grabbed her coat. Isabel sat on the bed, gripping her jacket tight, her knuckles white.

'Iz? Come on – I want to find these things and be done with it. Hurry up!'

'Elle… just think for a minute. I know I don't want to believe that this is happening, and I tried to convince you that it wasn't for a long time. I'm still not sure what's real and what's us freaking out and imagining things. But we could be about to do something really dangerous. You've found where the poppets are, and we know that some people believe that these are very powerful things. If they *are* binding the souls of those poor women to the earth – actually, I can't believe I just said that.' She rubbed her hand through her fringe, leaving it in small spikes. 'But if they *are* binding the souls of the witches, and the witch-finder – a *demon* for goodness sake – is after them, and will do anything to keep them in his power, answer me this: how can we hope to go up against that? It's not like we have special powers or anything!'

Eleanor sat down and put her arm round her friend. 'Izzy, this is something I have to do. I don't have a choice. But you do – you don't have to come. In fact, it might be safer if you don't.' She grabbed Isabel's hand and squeezed it. 'You've been great, but I don't want to put you in any more danger. Remember, I have the power contained in Ellenor's pendant – it's like a talisman. I have the pendulum to guide and protect me. I even have Ellenor's words to lead me. I'll be fine, honestly. All I have to do is find the poppets and destroy them.'

'*All you have to do*? What do you do for an encore, *superwoman*?' Isabel nudged her friend. 'Of course you need me! There's no way I'd let you go alone. I just wanted to say that we shouldn't rush into this. We need a plan of some sort.' She stood up and smoothed her hair with her hand. 'OK, we know roughly where we are looking. We need a couple of trowels in case we need to dig. I suppose we could go and have a look in daylight to see what we can find out, but we may have to go back at night to do any poking about – the education officer might object to us just churning the place up! Unless... hey! I've had a brainwave! I've suddenly thought of a use for one of the nerdy things you've dragged me into over the years. If we need to dig, we can flash these at the staff!' She rummaged in her bag and pulled out a small laminated card. 'I never thought I'd be glad to have a Junior Archaeologist membership! We can tell them we are working on a project!' She jumped up and grabbed her jacket. 'Come on – your mum will have loads of hand tools in the shed. I'm sure she won't miss a few for an afternoon!'

'Izzy – you are amazing. I'm really glad you're in this with me.'

After a quick stop at the shed in the garden, the girls were on their way back into town. As the bus pulled in next to St Dominic's, the girls jumped off and walked down the hill towards the river.

'Poo – you can smell the stables, can't you?' Eleanor coughed, holding her nose. 'We should go there some time. The indoor arena is supposed to be great!' The smile fell from her face as they reached the viaduct at the bottom of the hill. The shadows underneath were deep and cold, and they seemed to reach out towards the girls. They walked slowly towards the farm.

Isabel picked up a leaflet. 'Elle... have you got the pendulum? You should maybe use it again now on this map of the farm.' Eleanor nodded, and opened her backpack. She unfolded the leaflet carefully and sat on a wall. She held the pendulum above the map, and it began to spin. Slowly at first, then faster, it spun around the Ouseburn Farm site. Suddenly, it jerked towards the river.

'Izzy – I think it's pulling us behind the farm – maybe the river bank?' They walked under the viaduct and Eleanor shivered. The pendulum tugged and flicked in her hand. 'No – I don't think it's here... ' she sighed. 'Let's go back up by the entrance to the farm and start again. It was spinning properly there.' The girls walked away from the river, back up the steep hill and stood in front of the farm. Once again, the pendulum spun in a tight circle. 'Let's walk the other way.' They passed the entrance to the farm, and walked towards a tall, red brick building.

'The Cluny – my mum goes there sometimes to watch bands... she saw *Pale Man Made* there last week, remember?' Isabel nodded. 'You don't think the dolls are *under* the building, do you? We'd never find them then!' The pendulum leaped and tugged them down the side of the building.

'It's definitely pulling towards the river... ' Eleanor looked up. A narrow slipway between the Cluny and the farm led down to the muddy riverbank. The girls walked across granite cobbles slick with green algae.

'Careful – it's slippy!' Isabel cried as she slid across the walkway and banged in the wall. 'Ouch! Hey... this wall's really crumbly. The poppets could be hidden in there!'

'That's a good idea, Izzy – but I don't think the wall would've been here in the 1650s… ' Eleanor frowned, looking round as the pendulum leaped and jumped in her hand.

'Think about it though, Elle – you said that the witch finder has hunted for the pendulum 'down the ages' – well, he could have moved the poppets to keep them safe! Even if the wall wasn't here in the 1650s – the poppets still could be here!'

'Izzy – that's brilliant! Ellenor said the poppets had to be close to the bones of the witches to bind their spirits, but she didn't say they couldn't be moved!' Eleanor grabbed her friend by the arm. 'Come on – let's look.' She carefully wrapped the pendulum and put it back in her pocket. The girls stood at the bottom of the slipway. The water in the Ouseburn was low, and grey mud glistened in the sunlight. Eleanor bent and poked about in the sludge. She lifted a piece of worn brick, and tiny grey slaters pinged onto her hand. 'Ugh!' she shook her fingers and wiped them on her jeans. 'They can't be hidden in the mud – they'd probably rot.' She stood and looked down the river. 'Well, there's Seven Stories – you know, the book place? I'm sure that if they'd found witch poppets when they were redeveloping the building that it would have been in all the papers, so I guess they aren't there… same for the Cluny.' She frowned. She looked up at the building, and saw a tiny green metal door set into the wall. 'Shame it couldn't just be as simple as that… a door in the wall.' She bent forward and rubbed her hand across a clump of fern growing out of the crumbling mortar. A chunk of powdery stone fell at her feet. Eleanor spun round.

'Izzy – I think this mortar's loose! Have you got the tools?'

'Erm… Elle – if anyone sees us scratching away at this wall there'll be trouble!' Isabel passed the bag to Eleanor.

'I think we need to do anything we can to help – a bit of trouble for scraping a wall is nothing compared to freeing Ellenor and the others!'

'I know!' Isabel frowned. 'I just meant we need to be careful, that's all. Here – give me a scraper.'

The girls worked away at the loose mortar. It was paler than the harder, darker rock around it. Gradually, the large stone worked loose. Eleanor peered into the gap.

'I can't see anything... what if this isn't the place?'

A crow swept down from the viaduct. It called to the girls as it circled them.

'Corvus! Well – I guess that sorts that one then – this has to be the place!' The wind whipped at her hair, blowing it into her eyes. As she brushed it away, her fingers left a muddy grey streak. 'Hey, Izzy – that wind's getting up. Have you got a spare hair bobble?'

'Of course – emergency cosmetic supplies always available!' Isabel pulled a pouch from her bag. She handed Eleanor a hairbrush and bobble. 'Actually, I'm going to put my jacket on – I think it's getting cold. Must be because we are down by the river...' she shivered. By now, the wind was ruffling the water. It lapped against the bank, making tiny slapping sounds as it hit the mud. The sky had darkened to a grey metal, heavy with the promise of rain.

'We'd better hurry.' Eleanor tied her hair and scraped at the mortar once again. She wobbled the stone experimentally. 'Hey – it's moving! Give me a hand, Iz!' The girls worked the heavy stone up and down as the crow circled lower and lower, cawing excitedly. It landed on the top of the wall and hopped from foot to foot.

'It's coming… ' A dark shadow passed above their heads. Eleanor's head snapped up, but it was just a leaden cloud blocking the sunlight. Crumbs of mortar skittered across her foot, like spilled sugar. The stone lurched forwards.

'Oh! I think we've done it!' Heavy raindrops began to spot the ground with dark splashes.

'And just in time!' Isabel helped Eleanor to ease the stone out of the wall. They peered into the dark gap left behind.

'There's something there, Iz! It looks like fabric.' Eleanor rammed her hand into the hole and tugged at a fold of soot-stained sacking. The material was still wedged into the wall. Eleanor pulled again, gritting her teeth. The fabric tore, and a pile of lumpy brown dolls tumbled down the wall, onto the damp floor.

'It's them! The poppets!' Isabel hissed. 'Quick, Elle – before they get soaked.' She scooped the dolls into her bag as the rain got heavier. Drops drove down hard into the river behind them, making grey lines like shards of glass as they hit the water. Thunder rumbled in the distance. Eleanor pushed the stone back into place.

'We'd better get inside.' Eleanor flapped the sodden leg of her jeans. 'There's a café in Seven Stories – we can get a warm drink and have a look at them in there.' The girls rushed up the hill away from the river. By now, rain was running between the cobbles in rivulets. 'Come on – this rain's awful!' They charged into the building, and the receptionist raised an eyebrow.

'Caught in the storm, girls? The cafe has a hot chocolate special on at the moment – and you look like you could use it!' Outside, wind buffeted the doors, and rain beat against the glass.

Eleanor stared into the gloomy street.

'Thanks! We could do with something warm!' Isabel smiled. She pushed Eleanor towards the lift. 'What's wrong with you?'

'I thought... I thought I saw someone watching us.' She shivered. The lift arrived and the doors opened with a *ping*.

'I'm sure it was nothing. We're scaring ourselves now!' she rubbed Eleanor's arm. 'It's bright and warm in here, and there's the promise of a discount hot choccy to come. What could go wrong? There might even be marshmallows!'

Eleanor smiled weakly. The lift shook, and lurched to a halt. The light strobed and then flickered out.

'Izzy... ?' Eleanor reached for Isabel's hand in the darkness. 'Your hand is so cold! Are you OK? What do you think happened? I'm sure there must be an emergency button on the wall here somewhere... ' She groped forwards, still holding Isabel's hand. 'You must be a bit chilled – your hand feels really icy! If I could just find – Oh!' Eleanor had expected to find the cool metal wall of the lift in front of her. Instead, her hand felt a rough, damp surface. 'It feels like... stone! That can't be right. What's happening? Izzy – are you OK?' She tugged at Isabel's hand. As she squeezed, something dug into her fingers.

'Ow! Are you wearing a ring? Talk to me, Iz. I know this is scary, but... ' she reached out her other hand to touch her friend, and grabbed a handful of rough woollen cloth. A strong hand grabbed her wrist, wrenching it away from the fabric. Light flared suddenly, and Eleanor found herself staring into the black eyes of the witch finder himself. His face was inches from hers, and his icy breath swept across her cheek as he spoke.

'*Witch, you are mine. If you hand the poppets to me now, I may yet spare you.'*

Eleanor shrieked, and jumped backwards, hitting her head hard against the wall. Warm blood trickled through her hair, and she raised her hand to her head. Her eyes closed with pain.

'So anyway, once we've had this hot chocolate I want to go back up into town to Eldon Square if that's OK with you. I want to do some window shopping because Mum said she'd get me a new outfit for my birthday. Elle? Are you listening?

She opened her eyes to see Isabel staring at her. The lift juddered to a halt and the doors opened at the cafe. She pulled her hand away from her head and looked at it.

'There's no blood... ' she muttered. 'It's just wet from the rain.'

'Hmm? What was that Elle? Yeah – my hair's wet too.' Isabel flicked her fringe. It's not the end of the world though. We can stick our heads under the hot air blowers in the loos!' The girls walked towards the counter. Eleanor looked back at the lift, frowning. The doors slid shut, and she rubbed her face.

'Iz – something weird just happened in the lift. It was like I wasn't *there* with you any more – I was back in that room at the Keep – the one where we saw the blood stains. I banged my head. And I grabbed hold of someone – but it wasn't you. It was the witch finder. He wanted the poppets back.' She rubbed her arms to warm herself. Isabel spun round and gaped at her.

'I thought you spaced out a bit there. I was talking to you, and you were staring at me, then you put your hand up to your head. I just thought you weren't listening. Elle, I don't like this. It's like he's reaching towards us from the past.'

'Well, whatever he does, he's not having these poppets. We

know how important they are. I think we have to destroy them as soon as possible, and set those poor women free. But I'm not sure how we should do it.'

'You sit there and hold onto those dolls! I'll get the drinks, and then we can decide what to do. Back in a sec!'

Eleanor found a table in the corner. The cafe was nearly empty. A woman with a small child sat reading a book and eating biscuits, and a woman tapped away at the keyboard of her laptop. *It all looks so normal* she thought as she sat down. She glanced round the cafe again before she pulled the poppets from her bag. She looked down at a handful of grubby cloth dolls. Each figure was very simple, and they were all slightly different. As she handled the poppets, the pendulum warmed on her neck.

'Well – they're a bit of a let-down!' Isabel grumbled as she sat down, sloshing a small pool of chocolate on the table. She licked her fingers. 'I was expecting something that looked like the real witches. Those are just lumps of cloth with arms and legs, really!' She reached out and took a poppet, holding it between her thumb and forefinger. She turned it over and put it back in the bag. 'They smell a bit musty.'

'So would you if you'd been walled up for a few hundred years!' Eleanor wrinkled her nose. 'Poor things. The dolls just *represent* the women, you know. I don't suppose it matters what they look like, really. Anyway – once we get rid of them they'll be gone and the souls of the witches will be free. You're right – we need to go up into town when we've finished these.' She rattled her cup and poked her finger into a sticky marshmallow. 'We need to ask Kelli about poppets – and how to free the witches!'

Chapter Seventeen

When they left Seven Stories, the rain had stopped. Grey clouds still hung overhead, and the sky pressed down heavily on the girls. They rushed up the hill and jumped on an orange bus into town. As it pulled away into the traffic, dirty water arced out in a bow wave that soaked the pavement.

'That was some downpour!' Isabel flicked water off her arms. Droplets of rain showered across the seat.

'Hey!' Eleanor squealed, pushing her friend. 'I'm wet enough already!'

They jumped off the bus at Eldon Square, and were soon standing in the front of the shop. The comforting, warm scent of patchouli wafted round them. Gentle pan-pipe music filled the store, and the girls saw Kelli.

'Hi girls! With you in a moment.' Kelli was serving a group of young girls who were buying small crystals. As they waited, Eleanor and Isabel looked at a shelf of incense sticks and herbs. Rhanna rushed into the shop holding a paper bag.

'Hi there! I must have known you were coming! I've just been out buying doughnuts.' Kelli finished at the till and came across to see them.

'You pop through and put the kettle on – I'll just tidy round then it's time to close up the shop for the day. Won't be long!'

The girls followed Rhanna into the kitchen. As she made tea, they told her about the poppets.

'Do you have them here?' she whispered, her eyes wide. Eleanor unzipped her bag and pulled out the dolls.

'Well – they don't look much, do they?' Rhanna picked up a doll and turned it over as she examined it. The beaded curtain jangled.

'If those are what I think they are, they might not *look* powerful Rhanna – but I assure you, they are. Are those poppets, Eleanor? They look very old. May I have a closer look?' Eleanor handed a poppet to Kelli. She took it gently and her breath caught sharply in her chest.

'Oh! These dolls are coated in darkness! They have been used for a bad purpose.' She put the doll on the table, and wiped her hands roughly on a tea towel. 'What do you know about them, girls?'

'Well, this is going to sound far-fetched – but please listen. I don't know where else to go for help.' Eleanor's eyes sparkled suddenly with tears. Kelli put her hand on her arm, and bent in closely to look directly into her face. 'I will listen with an open mind and heart. Don't worry, my dear – I am sure we can sort out any problems you are having, with a little time.'

'I'm afraid that's something we might not have!' Eleanor frowned. She chewed her lip and started to tell Kelli everything about the witch finder, and the manner in which he bound the spirits of the witches to the poppets. Kelli listened carefully, sipping fragrant chamomile tea. As Eleanor finished, she leaned forwards and lifted the poppets gently into a basket lined with fabric.

'Those poor women.' She closed her eyes. 'I shall do everything in my power to help you. I will not pretend it shall be easy, but I do know a little about the use of these things. In some magical traditions, poppets are made for positive reasons – for protection. Magick is not 'good' or 'evil', 'black' or 'white' – it is just magick. It is the purpose for which spells and castings are used that determines if they are positive or negative. Sometimes poppets are used by witches with dark intent. When a poppet is made, something from the person it represents is put inside the poppet. This is called a *taglock*. It creates a magical link between the poppet and the person it stands for. Strands of hair, nail clippings – even a photograph is sometimes used. I expect these poppets will contain something that belonged to each of the poor women.' She patted the basket and pursed her lips. 'The cords that you see wrapped round the dolls have been used to bind the witches to this plane of existence long beyond their time.'

Eleanor sighed. 'We need to destroy them, but we weren't sure how to do it safely, without causing any more harm.'

Kelli stood and walked over to the bookshelf. It was crammed with big leather books with crumbling spines, as well as wrinkled, well-used paperbacks and a few dog eared magazines. She picked up a small book with a worn brown cover and leafed through the pages.

'Some people bury poppets once they are no longer needed, but I think to destroy the link, you need to burn them, and scatter the ashes at the four quarters – north, south, east and west. You should think of something to say which shows your intent to free the women from the demon's control. As the winds carry the ashes away, they become part of the wider universe. Only then will the souls of the women be free to travel on to the Summerlands. We shall be glad to help you, girls.'

Eleanor and Isabel looked at each other. 'Well, yeah – we thought burning them might be the solution. Time for a bonfire, huh?' Eleanor cracked her knuckles. 'Let's get started.'

The girls stood in Eleanor's garden. Sunlight poured through the twisted branches of the apple tree, outlining the last leaves with gold.

'Mum! Is it OK if we light the fire pit today? Isabel and I er… we want to toast some marshmallows and make some s'mores, OK?' Eleanor called up the stairs.

'Well, OK – if you find out the logs and the safety lighter, and wait a minute I'll come down and light it. You'll have to promise to be careful and not mess about though. It's far too dangerous if you aren't sensible,' her mother called back. 'There are some wooden skewers in the kitchen drawer, and the marshmallows are in the cupboard above the pans. I won't be long.'

After a trip to the shed, the girls lugged the bag of logs and stacked them in the fire pit. They went to the kitchen and pulled out the bits and pieces they needed for their cover story. Eleanor's mother came rushing into the room.

'OK girls – go and find a few bits of tinder – there are some nice dry twigs by the compost heap, and we can get going! Take that bucket and collect some in there. Stack it like a wigwam on top of the logs, and stick a few of those firelighters in the gaps.' Isabel grabbed the bucket and they rushed down to collect tinder. Soon, the firepit was ready to light.

'Mum! We're ready!' Eleanor called. Her mother came out of the kitchen carrying a tray with three steaming mugs.

'Spiced apple juice – and biscuits, marshmallows and chocolate for the s'mores! I'm getting in the mood myself now – I might even stay out here with you!'

'No! I mean… yeah, of course.' Eleanor blushed.

'No – it's OK. I know when I'm not wanted!' Her mother put her hand against her forehead and sighed tragically. 'I've got work to do anyway. I'll light this and drink my apple juice and then will allow you to banish me back to my study so you can gossip about boys – on one condition.'

'Name it!' Eleanor began to nudge her mum towards the door.

'Hey! No need to be so keen to get rid of me. A girl could get a complex, you know! The condition is… you bring me a couple of s'mores. You've got my mouth watering just thinking about them!'

'It's a deal. Thanks Mum!' Her mother leaned forwards and ignited the flame on the lighter. She held it against the tinder, and the flames caught on a dry twig. They raced hungrily through crisp, twisted leaves, and soon the firepit was blazing.

'There you go, ladies. Remember to wait until the blaze dies down before you start your toasting though. And go and fill that bucket with water before I go inside. I like to know we have all bases covered in case of emergencies!'

'Fusspot! OK mum – won't be a minute, Izzy.' Eleanor soon came back with a brimming bucket of water.

'Sure you don't want me to add the fire brigade as a speed dial on my mobile?' she sniggered. Her mum batted her with the thick end of the lighter.

'Message received. But it's always better to be cautious, eh?'

'Yes Mum… of course. And we won't forget your s'mores.'

'I get the message. I am dismissed.' She sighed. 'See you later!' She took her empty mug and wandered back to the house.

'At last!' Isabel put down her mug. 'I was getting a bit worried there – you can just imagine it. *Oh, don't mind us – we're just burning these poppets to destroy an ancient evil and set a few women free. Enjoy the show!*'

'I know! I was sweating a bit there myself. Of course, now we need to make a few s'mores to keep up the story. Let's do it straight away.' Eleanor pushed the plate of marshmallows towards Isabel.

'OK – nothing like a bit of chewy sweetness to get a girl in the mood for banishing evil.' She smiled nervously. Isabel put six biscuits on a piece of foil, and placed a square of chocolate on each one. She popped a marshmallow on top of the chocolate squares and put the foil on the grill. When the marshmallow melted, she pushed a biscuit on the top to make a sandwich.

'They're ready!' Eleanor carried a plate in to the study. When she returned, she was carrying the bag of poppets.

'OK – here we go. Kelli said we need to sprinkle this salt she gave me in a circle round where we are standing to keep ourselves safe.' She quickly poured the salt on the ground. 'Ready?'

'Ready as I'll ever be… ' Isabel took a poppet from the bag and placed it gently on the fire. The girls continued until all of the dolls were piled together. Red and gold licked across the poppets, stroking their tiny, sad forms. First one, then another doll started to smoke, then caught light. Eleanor and Isabel watched as the ancient fabric blackened and singed before bursting into flames.

'It's unbearable. So sad to think that even after they died, after all that torture and abuse, they still couldn't rest. Those poor women were bound and tormented for so long – it's awful.' Isabel's eyes filled with tears.

'It's nearly over now, though.' Eleanor squeezed her hand. The smoke thickened and dark plumes rose above the fire pit, and stung their eyes. Isabel coughed.

'It's catching in my throat.' She grimaced. As the girls watched the flames engulf the poppets, the black smoke seemed to solidify.

'Elle? Can you see that?' A dark shadow twisted in the smoke, growing larger by the moment.

'What is it?' Eleanor hissed. A shape began to form. First fingers, then a hand reached out of the flames, grasping towards the poppets. It scuttled across the coals like an obscene spider, grabbing at the dolls.

'Elle – it must be him!' Isabel shrieked.

'Stay inside the ring of salt, Izzy! He can't touch us here.' She glanced nervously at the thick wall of white crystals that surrounded them. The four candle flames suddenly flared high, roaring like blowtorches.

'Elle! What's happening?' Isabel stared at the smoke hand as it abandoned the dolls and started to reach towards the girls. The pendulum around Eleanor's neck glowed brightly. She grasped it tightly and held it towards the fire pit as though it was a weapon.

Eleanor stood tall. She raised her hands and held them with her palms towards the fire pit. She felt cool hands guiding hers. As she opened her mouth to speak, another richer voice rang out.

'*Begone, foul creature! You cannot hurt us!*' she shouted. '*You no longer have a hold over me, or mine. Leave this place never to return. Your dark magick has no place here!*' She clapped her hands together and a shower of crimson sparks filled the air. They clustered around the smoke hand like a swarm of locusts, eating away at the darkness. Soon, the hand was laced with holes and daylight shone through. Eleanor waved her hand and gusts of herb scented wind dispersed the smoke. The fire had consumed the poppets, and all that was left were embers coated with a film of grey ash. Eleanor slumped forwards on the grass.

'Elle? Elle!' Isabel rushed to her friend, and helped her to a chair. 'Are you OK?' Eleanor rubbed her fingers across her forehead, leaving a trail of soot.

'I'm fine... wow – that was amazing. I felt Ellenor move *through* me. I could smell her spicy scent, and then I felt her power. It wasn't like she *took over*, exactly... she just made me stronger, and suddenly I knew exactly what to say.' Isabel stared hard into Eleanor's eyes.

'Has she gone now?'

'Oh, she's still here somewhere... I can feel her.' Eleanor wrapped herself round with her own arms.

'What about... him?' Isabel asked.

'I'd like to say he's gone,' Eleanor looked round the garden 'but... I'm not sure.' Isabel put her arm around her friend's shoulder.

'Come on, Elle. Let's go inside and get another drink. My throat's still all dry from the smoke. When the ashes have cooled, we can plan what to do next.'

Eleanor tapped her lips with her finger. 'I know what we need to do now. The ashes must be scattered at St Andrew's. They need to be with the witches' earthly remains.'

'Huh?' Isabel grunted.

'The bones, Iz. The ashes need to be sprinkled on the bones.'

Isabel made a strangled noise, deep in her throat. '*Elle*... ? A graveyard, old bones, those poor witches – it's all a bit grim. I feel like we've passed into some weird dimension... but it's hardly Narnia!'

'It's more like some sort of *Roman Dirge* goth-comic from *Travelling Man*.' Eleanor smirked.

'You and your comic book shops!' Isabel sighed heavily. 'OK then. If we are going to do this, we need reinforcements. Will you ring The Dancing Goddess, or shall I?'

Chapter Eighteen

St Andrew's churchyard was washed with moonlight. Frost spangled the tops of gravestones, making them sparkle with orange glitter as the streetlights shone down. Eleanor, Isabel, Rhanna and Kelli crept through the gates and walked quietly behind the church as they had planned. They could hear buses passing on Newgate Street, and people laughing and talking as they came out of the cinema at The Gate.

'I hope nobody sees us.' Eleanor whispered.

'I hope nobody *bites* us – it's all a bit *Van Helsing*, isn't it?' Isabel's eyes widened. Eleanor bent over and rummaged in her backpack.

'Have you got the bag of salt? I've got the candles... and the box of ashes.'

'Yes, I *have* got the salt. My Mum had a new box in the cupboard. I hope she doesn't miss it!'

'Right – can you spread the salt in a circle again? It'll have to be quite big. I'll set out the four candles.'

'I've brought saltpetre and some sage to add to the protective circle.' Kelli started pulling jars from her velvet bag. 'The saltpetre can be added to the salt ring – it repels evil and banishes negativity. I'll burn the sage before you say your piece, Eleanor. It will help to cleanse the circle before we start. I've bought the ring, too. I think we should bury it here, in a hole full of salt, wrapped in a binding spell.'

'I know after all that's happened, we have to be careful, but you don't really think that there's any danger of him coming back, do you?' Isabel said quietly. Her eyes searched the graveyard as she spoke. 'And I don't want to touch that ring, ever again.'

'I think he's gone for good this time. But we can't take any chances. We have to see it through, right to the end.' Kelli dug a hole in the peaty soil, and lined it with salt that sparkled like snow in the moonlight. She took a small package and placed it in the hole before covering it with soil and a cairn of tiny stones. As she worked, she murmured a spell of binding.

Eleanor walked round the circle, putting the candles in place and lighting them one by one. The light flared, and Isabel saw the flame reflected in Eleanor's eyes. As she stood up and stepped inside the circle of salt, she looked older, like a grown and powerful woman. Kelli lit a sage smudge stick and waved it round the circle, humming as she walked round the perimeter. The air grew warmer.

'Shall I get the ashes ready?' Isabel whispered. Eleanor nodded. She took the bag and put it on the ground at the centre of the circle.

'OK – here goes.' Eleanor took a deep breath.

'We have come here, at this time and in this place to remember the women hanged as witches on the Town Moor in Newcastle. Terrible though that was, we know these poor people suffered a worse fate after death at the hands of the shape-shifter. We have come here today to set their souls free for all time. The demon bound them to this earth with poppets so he could harness their power. We have destroyed the poppets, removing his control over them. Now we reunite the ashes with their poor, restless bones.'

She lifted the bag, and poured ashes into each person's hands in turn. Finally, she poured the last into her own palm. Each person took up their position next to one of the four candles. Isabel allowed the ashes to trickle through her fingers.

'I call upon the element of water to wash away your pain.'

Rhanna blew her ashes until they were caught and carried away by the breeze.

'I call upon the element of fire to burn away the shackles that held you here.'

Kelli threw the grey powder high and watched, smiling as it blew away.

'I call upon the element of air to lift up your souls and carry them to the Summerland.'

Eleanor scattered her ashes onto the ground.

'I call on the element of earth to take these ashes and bear you back to the body of the Mother Goddess, where you can finally rest.'

Suddenly, the air was filled with the scent of apples and cinnamon.

'Elle – oh, look!' Isabel pointed at the edge of the graveyard, at a gnarled old tree. Mist tinged with blue light sparkled in the moonlight, coiling round the trunk. It flowed just above the ground, tracing light beams across fallen leaves and stones as it moved.

'It's making a circle… ' Eleanor breathed. As the ends of the circle met, there was a flash and a wall of blue light shot up in the air. The column of light eddied inside like oil shifting on water, making patterns of mauve and green. Shapes wafted backwards and forwards like fronds of seaweed. As the girls watched, they saw the shapes forming faces, bodies, arms and legs. Long hair flowed and skirts billowed as the shapes became women, dancing in a circle, holding hands. They smiled and laughed silently as they whirled faster and faster. Suddenly, they raised their arms above their heads and beams of glittering light shot into the air, sparkling in the darkness.

'Can you see that... ?' Eleanor whispered. She looked across at Kelli, who was hugging Rhanna. Tears streamed down the woman's face. Isabel stared at the lights as they faded into the darkness.

'*Eleanor...* ' a voice called softly. She looked over her shoulder and saw a tall, red haired woman smiling at her. She was wearing a red girdle and a long green skirt which blew in a breeze Eleanor could not feel. '*You have done it, just as I knew you would. We are free at last. I thank you with all of my heart.*'

The woman looked down as a tabby cat rubbed round her legs, then jumped into her arms, scrubbing its head against her in ecstasy. '*Skitterpaws, my love! I have missed you so.*'

A crow flapped down from the tree and landed on the woman's shoulder. '*And Corvus. It feels so good to be with you once more.*' She caressed the silky feathers, and the bird closed his eyes happily, nestling its head into a coil of her hair.

The woman looked at Eleanor, her face glowing. '*We cannot thank you enough. I must go now, but I know in my heart that we shall meet again. We are bound together by our duties as guardians of the pendulum – and we are bound together now by our love for one another. Thank you.*'

Ellenor's image started to fade. Gradually, as Eleanor watched, moonlight passed through her and lit up the scene. First she could see the tree trunk, then the stone wall through the image as it thinned, and winked out.

Eleanor ran to Isabel and threw her arms around her friend.

'We've done it! They're free!' The girls hugged and laughed. Rhanna and Kelli rushed across and joined them.

'You should be so proud, girls – all of you. You have achieved something wonderful here.' Kelli turned to Eleanor. 'And you, my dear, will have to take special care of that pendulum now. We know the power it holds, and we know the darkness it attracts.'

Eleanor's hand flew to the pendulum. It still hung round her neck on the delicate chain. It felt warm in her hand.

'Kelli… it's glowing again.' She whispered. Her eyes darted around the misty graveyard.

'Don't worry – it's bound to be, what with all the magick that has passed through this place tonight.' Kelli put her arm round the girl's shoulders. 'Come on – let's get you all home. We can talk about all of this tomorrow.'

As the group walked towards Kelli's car, a shadow shifted. It slipped out of the depths of a cracked tomb like a snake. As it slid across the mounds that covered the long-dead, the grass blackened. Wind whipped dry leaves to whirl into the sky, and Eleanor was buffeted back by a gust of freezing air. Isabel caught her arm as she stumbled away from the car door.

'Steady! Did you trip?' she asked.

'I… I felt as though I was being pushed.' Eleanor whispered. She looked over her shoulder, her eyes sweeping the gravestones. 'Just the wind… I'm sure it was just the wind.' She pulled her coat tightly around herself.

As the car drove away, a dark figure bent over newly turned earth. Pale hands scraped at the soil, scattering white crystals across the ground. Bony fingers curled round a tightly bound parcel. Hungrily, yellowed nails clawed at the paper, revealing a ring bearing an emblem of crossed keys. The moonlight bathed the ring in silver light, before powerful fingers clamped shut, smothering it in darkness.

Witchy Words

Ague – An old-fashioned name given to a feverish illness causing chills and shaking

All Hallows – Halloween or Hallow'Een (31st October). Also called Samhain or Samhuin. This is the pagan equivalent of New Year, a festival of new beginnings and fresh starts. The worlds of the living and the dead are supposed to find it easier to communicate with each other at this time.

Aventurine – A semi-precious gemstone, which is usually coloured green.

Banish – If a witch banishes something, she is magically ending or exorcising it. If something is banished, it is removed.

Beacon – A signal given to guide somebody. A bonfire on a headland could be a beacon for ships to follow, for example.

Besom – A traditional broom made from brush or twigs, used by witches when casting circles and some spells.

Beltane – Beltane (or Bealtaine, or Bealltainn) is a festival at the beginning of May, which celebrates the beginning of the summer. Like Samhuin, it is seen by pagans as a time when the Otherworld is particularly close at hand.

Binding – To magically stop something or someone from doing harm to themselves or to others.

Blessed be – A saying used by witches which may be used as a blessing, or to say 'hello' or 'goodbye'

Channelling – When a person receive 'messages' from a 'teaching-spirit' or ghost - and the ghost communicates with others by using a living person to 'talk' for them. In the story, Ellenor is channelled by the modern day girl, Eleanor.

Circle – In witchcraft, a circle is 'cast' or marked (with a wand or knife, or drawn in salt or chalk) to contain energy and form a sacred space. The circle acts as a form of magical protection.

Citrine – A yellow semi-precious stone.

Divination – Divination is a way of finding out about things - including events in the past and future - using magical tools. Tarot cards, crystal balls and runes are examples.

Dream catcher – Dream catchers are decorations with a net at their centre. They were first made by Native American or First Nation people, but have more recently been used by New Age groups. They are used as a charm to protect sleeping children from nightmares.

Element – Witches use the four elements during rituals: Earth, Air, Fire and Water. Many Witches add Spirit to this category. Each element has a direction that is used within a magic circle: East for Air; South for Fire; West for Water; North for Earth and the centre for Spirit.

Evil eye – The old belief that a curse could be put upon someone by 'overlooking' them - by glaring at them.

Familiar. – An animal with a spiritual bond to a witch, such as a cat, crow, dog - or even a toad, hare or ferret! The familiar is a magical creature that helps the witch in her work

Goddess – The female pagan deity, along with the (male) Horned

God. Some witches only worship the female Goddess.

Green Tara – A goddess called upon to help people to overcome fear.

Incense – Scented cones or sticks which release fragrant smoke when they are burned. Often used by witches during rituals.

Labradorite – A pearly grey semi-precious stone.

Lady of Avalon – High Priestess on the mystical holy isle of Avalon (now Glastonbury) at the time of King Arthur. Marion Zimmer Bradley wrote a famous book about the priestesses on the holy isle.

Magick – the art of focussing your will and emotions to make changes in the world. In the book Ellenor uses magick to cure people and to hurt the witch finder. He uses magick to bind the souls of witches. The 'k' at the end shows this is not the same as 'magic' tricks, such as pulling rabbits from a hat.

Malachite – A dark green semi-precious gemstone.

New Age – A description given to a variety of beliefs or practises including the use of crystals for healing, alternative therapies such as reiki etc.

Old Nick – A name given to the Christian 'Devil' or evil being; the opposite of God in Christian thinking.

Omen – A sign that tells of the future. An omen may be 'good' or 'bad.' At the time of The Black Death (the plague), for example, comets in the sky were supposed to have warned of the coming of the plague.

Pagan – followers of nature or earth-based religions such as witches, druids and wiccans. Pagan comes from the Latin word paganus, meaning 'country dweller'.

Pendulum – A pendulum is a crystal or other object that hangs from a string, cord or chain. In witchcraft, a pendulum is used as a tool for finding things - including the answers to questions. The pendulum is thought to make a collection with the mind of the person using it; it is also seen as a way of connecting to spirits.

Phooka – According to legends, a phooka is a huge dark coloured animal that may take the form of a rabbit, goat, dog or horse with glowing yellow eyes. It allows people onto its back, taking them for a wild ride.

Poppet – A poppet is a doll made to represent a person, for casting spells that will affect that person. Poppets can be made from roots, fruit, paper, wax, a potato, clay, or cloth. The poppets in Walking with Witches are made from cloth.

Poultice – A poultice is a soft, heated material put on sore or inflamed injuries. The word poultice comes from the Latin word pultes, meaning porridge!

Psychic – Psychic means to see things hidden from the ordinary senses of smell, sight, taste etc. by the power of the mind.

Shape-shifter – A shape-shifter is a person or creature which can change their physical form or shape. A werewolf is a typical shape-shifter. In *Walking with Witches*, the witch finder is an ancient evil being who took the form of a shape-shifter to persecute witches.

Sigil – A sigil is a symbol created for a specific magical purpose.

Summerlands – The Summerlands is a name given by some pagans to their afterlife or 'Heaven.' Some pagan people also see it as a beautiful place to rest between incarnations (lives).

Taglock – A taglock is a part of the human body used to attach a ritual or spell to a particular person. Common taglocks include hair, fingernail clippings or a drop of blood.

Tarot cards – Tarot cards have symbols which are used or 'read' to gain understanding about current and possible future situations.

Tincture – A tincture is a medicine made by soaking herbs in alcohol to extract the goodness.

Vision – A vision is a way of describing something someone 'sees' in their mind's eye, which helps them to make sense of a situation.

Witch finder – A witch finder was a person who travelled from town to town 'exposing' witches, who were then tried and killed if found guilty. Most witches in England were hanged rather than burned at the stake as seen in films and stories. Matthew Hopkins was a famous witch hunter during the time of the English Civil War, when *Walking with Witches* is set. Witch finders earned a great deal of money as they 'examined' men and women accused of witchcraft. The witch finder that came to Newcastle Upon Tyne in 1649 earned 20 shillings per witch – and that was a great deal of money when labourers were only earning six pence a day for their work!

Witch's marks – The witches' mark (also called a Devil's mark) was supposed to show that a person was a witch. The mark was believed to be made by the Devil to seal their obedience to him. He created the mark by raking his claw across their flesh, or by making a blue or red brand using a hot iron. Witch finders used pins to poke birth marks to 'prove' they were the mark of a witch, as the marks were supposed to be numb.